MW01232346

Also by Roy Luna:

The Squatter

A Revolutionary Education, a trilogy:

Part 1: *Lord of Reason*

Part 2: *The Exploits of Zénobe Bosquet, a Virtuous Young Atheist,
& of Monsieur Wagnière, His Fellow Librarian*

The Madwoman

The Madwoman

by Roy Luna

Poetry by Iris Cornelia Starkaugen

SOL⏝TION HOLE PRESS

SOL〰TION HOLE PRESS

First Edition
First Printing: 2019
ISBN: 978-0-9981712-3-4
Solution Hole Press LLC.
www.solutionholepress.com
Book & Jacket Design: Rowena Luna, LeftRight Design, Inc.
Front Cover photography: Abby Peña on Unsplash
Author photo courtesy of Rowena Luna

To Rowena Lily Luna,
kid sister, architect, engineer, artist, graphic designer,
photographer, feminist, environmentalist,
and the list goes on...

Foreword

We read poetry in a form very different from the reading of prose.

The narration of prose carries us like a stream to the sea, slowly at first, then it picks up momentum, presses us on through the mad dash of rapids and drops us without warning down relentless waterfalls, leaving us swirling in turbulent pools before we're dashed to the denouement.

Books of poetry, of course, may be just as thrilling, but we do tend to read them differently. First of all, each poem might be isolated and surrounded by the margins of a single page. Each poem is usually self-contained, although perhaps still thematically aligned with the rest of the collection. Poetic language forces us to read more slowly, more carefully, more diffidently, as we mull over the vocabulary, deliberate over connotations, identify the allusions, seek the echoes of metaphor and symbolism, savor the imagery, the pull of the provocative, the enticement of the phrasing.

This is why Iris's poetry, or rather, the bulk of it, will be found at the end of this book. A few individual poems are included in the main text to serve as exemplars of what she was writing during that time. But the editors did not wish the reader to experience a syncopated rhythm, an arrythmia of sorts, going back and forth from prose to poetry. It is to be hoped that the curious reader will, at the end, take full measure of Iris's poetry; it is, after all, the essence of this book.

Chapter 1

She walks the streets of Miami Beach exchanging bits of poetry for bits of food.

The booksellers at Books and Books on Lincoln Road Mall give her good paper so that she doesn't have to write her poems on paper bags, napkins, or strips of birch bark.

She hasn't seen the front façades of hotels for years, but she certainly knows their kitchen exits in the back alleys. There the staffs make sure she gets nutritionally-balanced meals with protein and carbs, and always desserts, for she is known to have a sweet tooth, but which unfortunately have caused most of her teeth to decay away.

As far as hobos, derelicts, and tramps go, she doesn't smell bad, she does not look menacing, and she does not glare at people when approaching them. Yet, neither does she smile. Somewhere in her past there must have been lessons in deportment, style and grace. Should she be menacing or aggressive when asking for handouts, she wouldn't get much, would she? By the way, she doesn't call them handouts; she calls them financial support for the arts. Even when on the dole, one must keep one's status and dignity. One's professionalism can never be in doubt. In exchange for subsidies, she hands out little treasures of her own: bits and pieces of poetry, which she calls her testament.

No one knows exactly what she means by that. Does it represent her testament as a witness to some act or circumstance, or her testament as a testator who leaves a legacy? Perhaps, in her mind, she means both at the same time? She sees; she testifies; she bequeaths. But perhaps, to her, the poetry she writes has no legal significance at all. Similar to a religious witness who can give firsthand accounts of the Lord's presence upon earth, she delivers witness of the grace of poetry and the power and the beneficence of literature upon all mankind.

She never speaks to strangers, however, so those bits of paper are the only testament to what goes on in her mind. After having given their bit of charity for the progress of the arts, the passersby graced by Iris glance at the bits of paper they have received, identify the text written on them as poetry, and, more often than not, probably out of curiosity, more than anything else, read the writing as they traverse the parking lot to their cars, or as they weave their way to the beach, or as they stroll on Collins or Washington in the early evening looking for a good place to eat.

A few tourist guidebooks and quite a few travel blogs have included the poetry bag lady in their chapters of interesting things to see and do in Miami Beach, almost as if a chance encounter with her is worthy of a sentence or two posted on Facebook so that the folks back home, especially those in Europe or Asia, can know two things: that there are vagrants—lots!—in America, and that there is such a creature as the Poetry Bag Lady of Miami Beach.

I met her through a mutual friend who lives on the Beach. George is a mathematician who teaches at a local college, and apparently he appreciates poetry as well because he had accumulated a little collection of her slips of paper on the mantle over his non-functioning fireplace. (With the earth warming up, who needs a fireplace, especially in Miami Beach!) George loves to go to Books and Books, and never cooks at home, so he has plenty of chances to encounter the bag lady on her peripatetic ramblings all over the southern part of the island.

I espied the poems on the mantle, probably because they were written on pieces of paper of irregular size and shape. Depending on the length of the poem, the bits were either squares or rectangles, although, since they seemed to have been carefully torn by hand, most were either trapezia or rhombi. The handwriting was clear, in elegant cursive, with effusive little loops at the ends of some words, especially those ending in a g, y, or z. The poems were written in different colors of ink, pencil, even charcoal, but one was written in what probably had to have been tree sap, or flower secretions. I remember as a kid making careful illustrations on my Dad's white Pontiac LeMans with the honey extruded from the flower stems of Surinam cherry bushes, for which I was paid handsomely with a swift kick to the ass. They were also good to suck on, red, tangy and sweet, to go with my tears of rejected artistry.

George told me about her as I glanced through her literary compositions. I was impressed by both his descriptive commentary and the poems in my hand. Through the couple of years that he had known her, George had managed to collect a few facts about her life. She had a name. It was Iris Cornelia Starkaugen. She came from the German petroleum family, the Starkaugens of Frankfurt, but she had been born in New York after one of the family's scions moved to America to try to escape the family business. There they set up their own business of bakeries and pastry shops, which explains why Iris had such a sweet tooth. Why she came down to South Florida is clear, but why she ended up back here is a bit murky, as are the reasons of most people who emigrate to South Florida. Most people who emigrate to North Florida have clear, precise reasons to move and remain there, for years. Not so for those who come to the southern part of the state. Most of them are fleeing something. Political and/or economic instability in their native lands; bankruptcy up north (no one can take your home away in Florida); state income taxes elsewhere; marital strife;

unemployment; reality. They live here for a while where they encounter our reality and then soon enough they come up against something in South Florida they need to flee. Especially those who choose to live in Miami Beach where transience, evanescence and evasion remain, as always, a decadent form of art.

Apparently, she came to school here, having been among the very first class to receive diplomas from the newly-fledged Florida International University, back when there were only three buildings, Primera Casa, Deuxième Maison, and Viertes Haus. Why Third House was skipped is testimony to the chaos and bewilderment that reigned during those first mythical years. The library was excellent in some fields of study, but totally negligent in others. There were no dorms. There was no cafeteria. There was no auditorium. There wasn't even a pool. The first commencement ceremony of 1973 took place in the reading room of the library. (Before anyone takes me to task, I must declare that FIU today is an excellent university that has finally, fully, and plausibly grown into its appellation of "international." I should know; I was Class of '77, but I didn't stick around to get my undergraduate degree. Back then, FIU was far from "international," rather more like "Florida Cracker yokel." I preferred to do my senior year at the University of Miami, known then as now as "Suntan U.")

Iris took her diploma and ran. Where she went, nobody knows, not even her family. Apparently, running away was prevalent in this branch of an otherwise stolid Teutonic genealogical tree. She learned a few languages along the way, all due to the language of her current boyfriends (and at least one girlfriend), giving new credence to the maxim that a foreign tongue is best learned on the pillow, although in some of her cases it was probably a hammock. There was a boy from Mexico (Spanish); one from Martinique

(French); a young man from Latvia whose father was Cuban (Spanish again, and Russian); a genteel lady from New Orleans, her parents' executrix (French again, and Cajun); and, in mid-life, a man from Haiti (French once again, and Creole). This last one ended in real tragedy. He was a taxi-driver and very late on the way home from her house he picked up a last fare who shot him for his money. The miscreant was so drug-addled that he left the money in the cab.

To Iris's polyglotism, one must add a life-long love of poetry, for she wrote constantly, fervently, religiously, never letting up, never surrendering this obsession to any thing or any one. Through lovers and places, through calamity and hardship, she never put her pen down. Poetry flowed from her like honey down a wrecked beehive.

In the late seventies and early eighties she published two books of poetry. I was able to track down first editions of them through Abebooks, one in New York, where both were published, the other one in Colorado. (God, but books travel!) They were thoroughly enjoyable. I was pleased to discover that they were paeans to her loves and to her travels. They were mostly in English, but reverted now and then to the other languages she knew. Her writing was polyglot, polyamorous, and polyvalent. Her wanderings in her travels and in her emotions generated a type of poetry that was as thermodynamic as it was opulent in its exoticism of place and of sentiment. It was Claude Lévi-Strauss's thirst for the exotic in *Tristes Tropiques;* it was Rimbaud's delirium of *Une saison en enfer;* it was Asturias's surrealist interpretation of the Mayan creation myths in *Leyendas de Guatemala*. It was unsparing in its depiction of savage passion. It was unwavering in the force of its epiphanies. In the middle of a jungle, within view of a jaguar and its kitten, she recalls a battle of love in a towering ceiba tree where the semen and the sap flow and fuse like glue that attaches the lovers to the branches.

But this Daphne enclasps her fair Apollo to her bosom and hence to her fate. Their bodies sprout leaves as from their hair emerge the silk-floss flowers. They fuse with the ceiba and in nine months her fruit drops to the ground to be devoured by creatures of the night who take the seeds in their gut to a new spot in the jungle, there to shit them out. Slowly the kernels sink in the damp earth and sprout and give birth to her children, the tree-children who can see things in the forest that men cannot. A crop of infant-plants who grow to see clearly in the gloom of the understory and in the dappled shining of the canopy. This vision of seeing more, farther, and better than others becomes a theme in her books. It is the vision of the arborescent child, in love with nature but at the same time part of nature, not having cleaved off of it, like man. It is in the spirit of the tree-hugger, only Herculean in its strength, militant in its intensity, succulent in its sensuality.

Iris Cornelia Starkaugen was a force of nature, in her younger days. What she had become in the present was a mystery. How could so much energy have been sapped, and to such a degree, that she now wandered aimlessly around the streets and alleys of Miami Beach, submissive as a leaf blowing in the wind? Where did the power of her youthful poetry flee? In what condition was her mind that she thought giving away her scribbles was optimum in its effectiveness?

By the way, thematically and stylistically, this latest batch of poems that Iris was scribbling and giving away to passersby was very different from those in her previously published books. No more forests, no more wild animals; now it was less lyrical, more urgent, intended to make people react.

A colleague of mine, Clara Estrella, and I had just founded a publication company, Solution Hole Press, with the intent of finding lost voices from the past and resurrecting them to a new audience. Iris was a poet I wished to pursue. Starting with those very first poems that George had in his possession, which killed me, I began to lust for more. Iris forced me to become a stalker. I lurked in the shadows of trees. I loitered under bridges and behind walls in backstreets. I sank to the ground to blend in with sand dunes. I followed Iris around, without her noticing me. Every time she succeeded in handing one of her pages to a passerby, I accosted the individual to ask if I could please take a picture of the text. More often than not, they just quickly handed the paper over to me, apprehensive of my motives.

I ask myself why I chose this mode of operation. Why not have solicited Iris directly and asked for her cooperation in the publication of her latest poetry? After all, she wasn't a wacko; she was rather nice. Her eyes didn't seem to focus on her interlocutor's eyes, but rather saw things behind him. This was a bit unsettling, but one of my cats does the same thing. Lucy looks beyond me, or rather, through me, and her eyes follow an activity to which I am not privy. Of course, she knows I'm there for she responds to me. But she witnesses something else which I cannot even begin to perceive. Like Lucy, Iris watched a world that was wider and deeper beyond what we mere human mortals could fathom. But it took me a while to hatch the following thought: perhaps it was not otherwordly activities that they were observing during the time I was there. Perhaps they were viewing activities that had happened in that same spot, but at other times, either in the past or in the future. What they looked on was not somewhere else; they were somewhen else.

Something about what I know of the homeless, of the paranoia that grips a lot of them in their day-to-day lives, kept me from confronting her. Eventually, I knew, I was going to become one of the passersby, intentionally. I would then continue to cross her path a few times a week. It would mean spending more time on the Beach than I would have liked, but, hey, for the love of literature a man is willing to do many things. So long as I steered clear of the island on the weekends when traffic grinds to a halt and even the swift sea breezes cannot sweep the exhaust fumes away fast enough, it could be palatable. I would also need to stay away during King tides when many of the streets are awash with sea water. There would be a plus, however, since I would also see George on a regular basis. We would have dinner together. We would see Iris as she floated gracefully about. We would give her a few dollars and in return receive her ratty pieces of paper with these magnificent bits of poetry written elegantly on them. I salivated to see more of her poetry. I saw in my mind a book of her poetry come to fruition, come to the light, and to the attention of a new generation. Solution Hole Press would do it, and Clara and I, Iris's editors, would reintroduce her to the world, and she would receive her rightful recognition, acclaim, perhaps adulation. Iris could perhaps get off the streets, live in a place of her own, nice and tidy. She could write on a computer or an iPad. She would have spell check!

My enthusiasm was great and my hopes high. I was going to befriend Iris. I was going to gain her trust. The entire world needed to discover her poetry, not just a few locals and tourists who happened to cross her way. All of humanity needed to see her poetry, for here was a new Cassandra, a new seer who, with her sight and insight and foresight and chronosight brought her remembrance of the past through the mindful present to trace the pattern of the future. But I feel I'm getting ahead of myself. I return to the first poems that I found in George's flat. There were a baker's dozen, a good sign, considering her family's business.

Here is the first of those. The rest will be found in the appendix.

once upon a time waits for no one time stands still stitch in time endless time after time and again time is of the essence time be still time flies lost time changes everything the time has come in the fullness of time illusion of time the great healer one more time there is a time and place time will tell the time is ripe in the nick of time is a river time on your hands a matter of time wasted time is the master love kills time time kills love spend time no hand to catch time the first time the last time take the time make up for lost time heals time destroys time and tide killing time no time like the present time and space the time has passed time past time lost time regained time recalled a race against time. time's up.

∞

Chapter 2

*G*eorge is a mathematician, taciturn and smart.

I don't know why he lives on the Beach. Perhaps it is because as a Cuban, he likes to be surrounded by breezes redolent of fish, seaweed, and belching flotsam floating up with each tide. Being of a type best described as circumspect or meditative, George does not partake of the loud, boisterous style of most of the residents of South Beach. There, life is typically fast, active, colorful, musical, much like a reef on amphetamines chased down with plenty of booze. I think George likes a glass of dry white wine with dinner.

I'm glad George is quiet and a bit diffident. Otherwise, he might not have become interested in the Madwoman of Miami Beach. He may indeed not even have noticed her. It is hard to notice a pedestrian when one is sliding by life in a convertible with the wind whipping your face as you go careening from club to club. At that speed, running into her would not have been possible; running her over would have been easier.

Still, at least for readers of literature, it is difficult not to notice Iris. She is straight out of the pages of a novel: Voltaire's lively old lady in *Candide* comes to mind. Beaten, defiled, one of her buttocks devoured by cannibals, she remains unceasingly a sprightly hag. Dickens's tomes have tucked into their pages a few extravagant elderly dames, resolute and eccentric, one of which could have been Iris. Villon's ancient helmet-maker's wife who counsels her fellow prostitutes could also be a sister to Iris for she too has a message to transcend the times. No longer able to attract the type of client that they can, la Belle Heaulmière reminds them that their youth and beauty are but transitory. Much too soon they will repel men what with their sagging breasts, shrunken arms, drooping shoulders and wizened faces. With age comes wisdom and she teaches them to prepare for that time of life.

La Dame aux Camélias she was not. *La Folle de South Beach* was much too active, covering kilometers of terrain daily. Iris's sobriquet was given her by a French blogger who had come across the poetess on Ocean Drive and 5th, and who, quite obviously, had read, or seen, Jean Giraudoux's play *La Folle de Chaillot*. Still, there's not that much comparison between Iris and Madame la Comtesse Aurélie, the play's protagonist, seeing how Iris was humbly an intellectual, and Madame la Comtesse was flamboyantly an entitled, albeit impoverished, aristocrat. Yes, they both represent the opposition to mercenary business interests that flay the earth open in order to get at her riches. They both fight to preserve the beauty and the health of our Mother Earth who succors us; they both abhor our past sins and hope for a better future. But Madame la Comtesse Aurélie harbored the timid hopes of a Panglossian optimist; Iris Cornelia Starkaugen is a realist, a Kantian idealist who believes that human reason will lead ineluctably to human progress, and a way out of our difficulties. Physically, Madame la Comtesse Aurélie was a pushy broad dressed in the anachronistic garments of a century earlier, held together by bobby pins and cobwebs. She was a feminist harridan who held court disguised as Miss Havisham.

But Iris has always had a style of her own, cobbled together by her travels and by her loves. Nostalgically, she always took to wearing long, flowing gowns, no matter how high the mercury, no matter how virulent the sun. Usually white or in pastel colors, they bespoke of a graceful past, perhaps as one might picture an antebellum New Orleans elderly belle, or a Bermudan queen in jubilee celebration. Colonial is a word that comes readily to mind. Also graceful, dignified, elegant. Blanche DuBois is a sister;

Amanda Wingfield a cousin. Or even better, she is Sebastian's mother in *Suddenly Last Summer,* as played by Katharine Hepburn, who incidently also played the role of the Madwoman of Chaillot. Iris Cornelia Starkaugen must have been a character in a play that Tennessee Williams never wrote.

Iris did stop at wearing gloves, however. No one in Miami ever wore gloves, I think. Sometimes she wears a hat of some sort, mainly to keep the sun from her eyes.

And what sun Miami has! Sweltering, blistering, yellow-white glaring sun. I go to England, France, Belgium or northern Italy in the early spring or in the late fall, because I envy those overcast, drizzly days when you can walk about without an umbrella since the drizzle evaporates as soon as it hits your body. On sunny days when Parisians hit their quays in partial garb, I visit cloisters and libraries, going deep underground into their cool, dark cellars.

In Miami, I run from air-conditioned house to air-conditioned car. Except for when I began to stalk Iris. I had no other choice but to loiter in the heat and oftentimes follow her unprotected under the sun. Like I said, the lengths to which I will go when chasing after literature surprise even me.

Through accosting people who had received snippets of Iris's poetry, I garnered a few more bits to add to her collection. Because of the recurring themes in the pieces, I began, at least in my mind, to call this collection *Le Déluge,* after Madame de Pompadour's immortal, and prescient, bon mot, *«Après nous, le déluge.»* Time, of course, was a major theme. As in, humanity had no more time. Destruction also fit in, as in end of times, apocalyptic, diluvian. I began to place the poems in different dossiers, each denoting a major theme. There were those, of course, that were difficult to place under just one classification. Then there were a few that fit no classification whatsoever. Those, as George rightly pointed out to me, were mathematical in nature, and mostly about the distortion of time. We didn't know how Iris came by her mathematical knowledge, but if the claims she made in her pieces were to be believed, it was her lover, Kronos, the god of time, who provided her with the calculations. Math is necessary in the reckoning of time, the making of calendars, the marking of the passing seconds. Just because the clock was winding down for humanity did not mean that time would in anyway cease to be or even be interrupted for a millisecond. The question remained, however, hovering over our lips. George and I looked at each other with some sort of alarm: would time even matter if man were no longer present to measure it?

All of a sudden, time would telescope once again into its original, paleontological dimensions, when entire eons would pass by, when millennia to the sixth degree would flash through a spinning earth. Centuries would be too small to concern oneself with. But one wouldn't be there. The short era of homo sapiens would be over, the evidence of an extremely transitory existence covered by seas and new volcanic effluvia, sliced by meandering tectonic plates to melt under magma.

Yet the equations would remain, perhaps to mark the universal structure of time, whether speeding up or slowing down. This particular detail was of no consequence to anyone any more. Was Iris concerned with what would happen to Kronos after he survived her?

$$\Delta t = M + \lambda p - \alpha$$

$$t' = t\sqrt{1 - V^2/c^2}$$

Where: t' = dilated time
t = stationary time
V = velocity
c = speed of light

$$m_0 \frac{d^2 r}{d\tau^2} = -GM_0 m_0 \left(1 + \frac{3L^2}{c^2 r^2}\right)\frac{r}{r^3}$$

$$dt_c \approx \frac{dt_E}{\sqrt{1 - \frac{2GM_E}{R_E c^2} - \frac{2GM_\odot}{r_E c^2} - \frac{v^2}{c^2}}}$$

$$\Delta\tau = \int_P \frac{1}{c}\sqrt{\eta_{\mu\nu}\, dx^\mu\, dx^\nu}$$
$$= \int_P \sqrt{dt^2 - \frac{dx^2}{c^2} - \frac{dy^2}{c^2} - \frac{dz^2}{c^2}}$$
$$= \int \sqrt{1 - \frac{1}{c^2}\left[\left(\frac{dx}{dt}\right)^2 + \left(\frac{dy}{dt}\right)^2 + \left(\frac{dz}{dt}\right)^2\right]}\, dt$$
$$= \int \sqrt{1 - \frac{v(t)^2}{c^2}}\, dt = \int \frac{dt}{\gamma(t)},$$

Her beloved Kronos fed her slices of time which she ate as if they were pieces of mamey or sapodilla or canistel, in other words, fruits that came from the Yucatán bulls-eye eons ago when the asteroid tore asunder the land and obliterated in concentric worldwide spasms the gigantic Jurassic creatures. They all died, all but the smallest of them, insects, birds and the newcomers, the mammals. The plants survived, evolved, begat flowers, attracted pollinators, increased the success rate of insects and birds, and their own germination. Eventually, from shrews and such, man came and, with his small attention span, time slowed down enough to be worth his measure of hours, seconds, milliseconds. Nature, however, ignored his tiny steps, his inability to grasp the changing eons, and escaped his attempts to manipulate the world around him over which he was never in control. Poor man! He thought he held time in his hand. All the time, he was being held, pinned like a dead beetle to a board. As far as nature was concerned, time was of no consequence, and man could not evolve fast enough to warrant being saved.

𝒟iluvium. Category of Apocalyptic poetry.

∞

I see things, disturbing things, when I look at you.

There's a cephalopod sitting on your head,
Inking your face, weaving its tentacles under your chin
Like a new Easter bonnet that pulses colors of neon;
Its molluscan foot anchors at the top of your skull
Where it drills to find soft tissue and feast on your brain.

You no longer remember your sin: you drilled through rock
Looking for fossil fuels that once were live tissue
And you took and you took till there was no more to take.
Then you found new violent ways to keep sucking like a leech;
You're so smart, now you wear the leech on your head.

It becomes you. It's you with electric hair. Its billowing tentacles
Search into your ears, slide up your nostrils, down your useless mouth.
There is food to be had in you. Up to the last second you denied
It was your fault; the torrents fell from above and seeped up drains,
Catapulted by rolling gushes across the sea to overtake the land.

"I am the victim here!" you howled, like the psychopath you are.
The water took you down. Lacking a conscience as you brought
Ruin to your home, losing memory of the crimes of your ancestors,
Faking blindness to ignore the wreckage of her whom you tore
To bits; her debris lying everywhere on land and sea accuses you, you, you.

"I am the victim here!" you insisted, as the water took you down.
Don't you know, you're punished for the wreck you made of your home.
But as I see you now, you're the wreck: but hey you look swell
With that bonnet on your head. You tilt your head this way and that,
As if admiring yourself in front of a mirror that isn't there.

∞

Chapter 3

Hovering around the Madwoman of the Beach was another eccentric derelict.

He called himself The Knife, but other than the threatening name there was nothing else about him that brought to mind the idea of a sharp blade. Quite the contrary. What is the phrase? He wasn't the sharpest knife in the cutlery? He also called himself Iris's *maquereau*, or pimp. I only ever heard him speak French. My powers of observation are great, but nowhere was there any idea that sexual commerce was being performed, nor was there any evidence of johns soliciting The Knife for Iris's prurient favors. The idea itself was ludicrous. Iris was a poetess. She was also too old for the oldest profession. She was a bit odd, to be sure, but one could tell that she was pure. There was, however, according to George, the startling fact that Iris shared with The Knife a certain percentage of the donations she garnered for the arts. Why she did this was a mystery: The Knife exuded nothing that could be construed as artistic, he did not help her write or distribute her poetry, and, to be candid, instead of attracting passersby to linger in the vicinity, he caused them to hasten their steps away from Iris.

It was my friend George who first told me about The Knife. Frequently, The Knife would come out of the shadows while Iris was giving George some of her poetry and confiscate the contribution to the endowment of the arts that George had just invested in her. It was his *pourcentage*, he announced. "I protect her." After he was gone, George would give Iris an addendum to offset The Knife's percentage. A bit bewildered, she would give George another of her poems.

As far as we could tell, The Knife was not protecting Iris very well. Often, he wasn't even around. We assumed he was just mooching off of her. But the percentages were trivial, and the society of tramps was enigmatic, so we did nothing about The Knife.

I realize that I am guilty of a huge literary faux pas. I have been prattling on about these people, i.e. characters in a story, and not letting you see them for yourselves. Still, these are real flesh and blood dramatis personae, and for the longest time I did not encounter them myself. In my mind, they were merely constructed by rumors and construed by hearsay. They came to my mind through snippets and vignettes told to me by George who is an excellent mathematician, but, alas, a mediocre storyteller. He tends to forget details which he adds at the end of major plot lines and as a result there is never a chronological continuity. He is constantly saying, "Oh, I forgot to tell you that..." and "Oops, I omitted to tell you..." and "Oh, you should know first that..." In addition, the first few times I met the Madwoman of Miami Beach, there was no dialogue at all. It was all gesticulation and mime. Facial expressions did not help since Iris saw all with the same listless countenance. It was as if her eyes couldn't really focus at all. She saw what was far away, her mien static and statuesque. Her immediate surroundings in the present were but an accident of her meanderings; only the future was of interest. Lastly, I myself am a horrendous chronicler, too disorganized to stitch together a story in true dramatic fashion, especially when it's a true story. My true stories read like my journal: nothing much happens, most of it is cerebral, dates are missing, chronology is suspect, time flows in a haphazard fashion. So, even if my memory might be spot on about what people say and how they said it, I may remain a bit fuzzy about when they said it.

In any case, here are the first few episodes of when I actually saw, and interacted with, Iris and The Knife.

The very first time, and I know it was the first time, George and I had just left the Mexican Restaurant El Rancho Grande on Lincoln Road Mall, and we were ambling back to his flat in The Rialto building on Ocean Drive between 14th and 15th Streets. In front of the Aqua Hotel on Collins, we caught sight of the lady in question wearing her long, flowing robes, walking barefoot, with bags made of cloth, paper, and plastic hanging from the crook of her arms, stopping people with one hand outstretched, the other clutching pieces of paper against her breasts. If people ignored her and sidestepped in order to pass her, she didn't insist, just went on to the next person. If, however, they gave her a contribution, she gave them a bit of paper. By this time, of course, George had already spoken to me at length about her, and I had already read the first batch of poems at his flat. In a few minutes, I realized, it would be our turn to receive her pieces of poetry. I felt a bit nervous as I took out my wallet in order to prepare my charitable offering. I took out a five-dollar bill. George, I saw, had taken out a less generous donation of two dollars.

When finally there were no other pedestrians between the Bag Lady and us, we sauntered on in as insouciant a fashion as we could muster. I even made it a point to admire the pink tabebuias in bloom along Collins, as if I were some sort of arboriculturist studying the flora of the Beach. I pretended to be surprised by a tall, thin lady standing in front of me, barring my way. George went first, since he had been accosted by her numerous times. He even bade her good evening, adding her name at the end with a friendly lilt. "Good evening, Iris." In exchange for his two dollars, she handed over a poem.

Then it was my turn. This is the moment I realized that Iris had beautiful blue eyes. They were the blue of an older person's eyes, a bit washed out, a bit teary, but still elegant and lovely. Her expression was blank, and she didn't focus on my face, but rather behind me, as I've already explained. She didn't look down as I placed the five-dollar bill in her hand, which was disappointing, for she didn't see how generous I was. I suppose I had been hoping to receive two poems from her, at least. She remained focused on where I had been twenty steps earlier, or maybe it was twenty steps into the future. Perhaps she felt tense at the immediacy of the present moment or the proximity of two people right in front of her. I smiled, hoping she'd smile back. I wanted to say something, but I couldn't think of what to say. As soon as she had placed the slip of paper in my hand, like a priest somberly pressing the host into my palm, she turned to look up Collins, floated across the street to meet the next passersby.

I read the poems on the spot, almost grabbing George's from his hand. I still hadn't begun to organize Iris's poetry, but later I recognized that they belonged to two of her favorite categories, submerged cities and Kronos. My first impression, however, was of simple admiration that a homeless person could write this well.

The poem I had received was short. It was written in her elegant script which gave testimony that there had been calligraphy lessons in her past.

∞

Jellyfish float among your bookshelves
Their projections open the pages
That undulate under waves;
Starfish knock tomes off
That float to new places;
The readers are long gone,
Their eyes blind to new stories.

∞

George's poem was a bit longer. It made me jealous, because it also was better, as if she had given it more thought.

∞

Poseidon does not exist
    Though his pet Kraken breathes through gills;
Neither does Hephaestus
    Though there are many men ugly as he;
Hypnos does not displace water or air
    For men fall asleep without him,
Just as they dream with no aid from Morpheus,
    Fall in love without Eros who has no heart;
Men die just as easily with no prompt from Thanatos
    who's not really there.
    But this I see, through bended refracted light,
That men are born, grow and die
    Under the hand of the one true god who does exist:
Kronos, god of time, the god who decides for us
    The accidents of our existence, the bifurcations
Of our destinies, and the events of our fates.

∞

We continued strolling, discussing the poems, digesting our dinners, casting unseeing eyes on our surroundings for we were deep in our deliberation. We got to George's flat by remote control; poetry may have dimmed our sight and spurned our steps, but it gave a lucid incandescence to our bookish analysis. Interpretation of Iris's poetry led us through ample strolls among language, significance, logic, and reality, with a vigorous foray into the irrational. It made me want to discuss our analyses with the poet herself.

The second time George and I saw Iris, I had the additional pleasure of meeting The Knife. George could not understand him, but Iris and I did. For the sake of the reader, I translate the dialogue into English, thus losing, unfortunately, the colorful and exotic exchange of a motley polyglot jargon. French as spoken by The Knife was an erratic, mostly erroneous pidgin, peppered with vocabulary borrowed from Spanish and English, whereas Iris's

French was a cultured and aristocratic version, as if delivered by Malherbe himself. (For those who have forgotten their French lessons, Malherbe was a Classic poet and theoretician who pushed perfection, simplicity, and purity of language.) I became, as in so many moments of my life, the reluctant translator, this time between the bilingual mathematician who spoke only English and Spanish, and the homeless polyglots.

"I don't want to go there," Iris was saying to The Knife as we approached them just before dusk on the parking lot of the Miami Beach Convention Center. (We had just left the Antiques, Art and Design show.)

"It only takes a moment," argued The Knife.

"I find only pain and anguish there. There is nothing for me there," came the unhappy reply.

"But it doesn't even hurt."

"My hurt lasts."

"But they pay us for our trouble."

"My trouble begins and lasts for days afterwards. To know that my blood serves to revive a person unknown to me, then I see that person in my mind very clearly, for we are forever joined by life's blood. That one person takes over my mind and he, or she, is the only one that I can see, sometimes for a very long time. It's the one person who does not allow me to see the other things, the things that affect all of humanity. All I see is the one, who sometimes dies, but sometimes lives. It's not until my blood is spent in his veins that I regain my ability to see general things, instead of the one."

"It is good for you to take a break between visions, anyway."

"I do not take a break. I agonize about the future of that one person. It is worse than the general visions I see. It becomes intimate, as if it were happening to me. People who need blood are at death's door. Sometimes they do not survive, and I'm released.

But sometimes they do survive, and I'm joined to them for as long as my blood courses in their veins, until my blood dissipates and is diluted by their own blood. I'm not going there. You can go alone."

"Come with me, anyway. You help to calm me down. I hate it when they stick the needle in me."

"I have to stay. I have many portents to give away today. They keep getting stronger and stronger. Time is running out."

"You've been saying that for years," said The Knife impatiently. "What's one more day?"

I had been translating into George's ear and he decided to interrupt their argument at this time.

"Good evening, Iris. Have you got a poem for me tonight?"

Iris swung around to identify the voice. She didn't smile when she recognized George, but rather looked wistful and empathetic, as if she knew with precision what horrible future awaited him. She reached into one of her multiple bags and produced a single square of paper. George handed her his two dollars after which she dropped the poem into the palm of his hand. She then automatically turned to me and stared through me.

This time I was prepared. "*Mademoiselle* Starkaugen," I said in French.

I don't know why I chose French. Perhaps it was on my mind because she had been speaking in French. Perhaps it was because French is a more elegant language that better serves the communication of fawning flattery. Perhaps it was because I didn't want George to understand what I had to say.

"*Mademoiselle* Starkaugen, I need to declare to you that I am in love with your poetry. I have read and reread every scrap of it that has fallen into my hands. I have tracked down the two books you published, read them cover to cover, and enjoyed every word. Your poetry is otherworldly, fraught with spiritual yearning, and I find it deeply inspiring. I would like to speak to you about the possibility of publishing another collection of your poetry, your latest poetry. I see you disseminate and fracture your work, most of it going into oblivion. I would like to collect it, capture it, publish it, so that others may enjoy it as much as I have."

I felt as if I were making an amorous overture, but it's true I did get a bit emotional. My earnestness must have impressed her for, although she still focused through my eyes, she knit her brows and approached me. She took my hand in both of hers, then the other, but only felt them. She didn't need to look at my palms.

"Oh, no," I heard The Knife say. "She's looking for your soul, *monsieur.* She's trying to follow your soul into the future. Perhaps you would prefer not to let her do that."

I wanted to answer him with a perfunctory *Pourquoi pas?,* but I didn't want to ruin the moment. I felt peaceful standing there with both my hands in hers. I was in a refuge of serenity, at this quiet moment, with darkness falling around us, cars leaving their parking spaces, the first stars appearing in the firmament. I saw all this with my peripheral vision. My eyes never left hers, although hers were looking past me. Such silence and peace are rare, as was the comfort I felt as she held my hands. But eventually she dropped them and they fell to my sides.

She rummaged through her bags until she found the right one. Then she took out a wad of papers and shuffled through those. Eventually she found what she was looking for. She held it up to me. It was a long one, I was happy to see. And she had chosen it for me. It was not random.

I quickly took out my wallet but as I opened it she applied her palm and forced my hand down. Wordlessly she offered me her poem. I took it as if receiving the sacred fire from Prometheus himself. I almost bowed to her, but found that the others might find that a bit ridiculous. Instead, I gently took her hand and brought it to my lips. I felt my eyes water and brim with tears. She had not wanted money from me. She had given me her poem for free.

She slowly turned away from us and floated down the sidewalk, her skirts ballooning behind her in the breeze. The Knife started to follow her. I called him back.

"*Monsieur,*" I asked him in French. "How much do they give you for donating blood at the blood bank?"

"They give me twenty-five dollars, and a free pass to the movies."

"Here's fifty. Now you don't have to go. *Mademoiselle* Starkaugen need not go, either. Please honor her wishes."

"*Merci, cher maître, merci bien,*" exclaimed The Knife. He turned to join Iris.

"Well," said George as we watched them walk away. "Are you going to tell me what that was all about?"

"Not until I have read these," I answered, absconding with the piece of paper in his hand and walking into the circle of light of the nearest streetlamp.

I read George's first, since now it was the shortest:

∞

> O my love is like a red, red barnacle,
> That's newly attached to me.
> O my love is like the anemone
> That's fast affixed to thee.
> Together we're held by tentacles
> That grip our bodies close.
> Crabs join claws like manacles
> That gird us like a rose.

∞

I guffawed when I finished reading it. I read it again, this time out loud. George laughed, too.

"I didn't know she had a sense of humor," he said.

Then I tore into mine, also reading it out loud:

∞

Paper, ink, and binding glue
    have withstood the test of time?
Parchment once, vellum, sheaves of papyrus reeds
    beaten to a pulp, even stone with deep carvings
Etched for a people not yet born, then buried, never found?
The books you call treasure are more delicate than gold or jewel
    for even a worm can with appetite gouge out tunnels:
It eats the words, digests their nourishing significance,
    rejects whatever indigestible truth remains.
Humidity mars the leather, foxes the pages,
    invites the silverfish to feast
Upon its voluptuousness.

Imagine how a flood will harm:
    Even if the waters are unhurried,
They engulf shelf by shelf, lap up sturdy bookcases
    Even when shielded by oaken doors and marred vitrines;
The water finds its way, to infiltrate, swamp and immerse them all;
The books avidly soak in the water long denied to its pages,
    like a good old friend returned from far away.
The books grow heavy, soggy, bloated, like gaudy
    new species of sea sponge that
Constantly slough off their skin.
    Sea beasts arrive
Quietly to feast on
    their
pulp.

∞

With mouth agape and a frisson down my spine, I handed the poem to George.

"This is the second poem about books! How did she know I like books?" I asked him.

"Well, I did understand that bit you mentioned to her about wanting to publish her poetry. I suppose that was a clue."

"Yeah, but, a lot of publishers today are quite happy to produce ebooks. I understand it's the newfangled way, but I still like the old-fashioned kind of books. How did she know I'm a bibliophile, and that this poem of hers would affect me to my core?"

George begged off the continuation of our discussion until after he had reread the poem for himself. I gave him the couple of minutes it took.

He turned to me and said something quite clever. "Look at the form the verses make. They sorta look like pages in a book. Don't you think so?"

I agreed.

"This is certainly a poem to blow a bibliophile's mind," George continued. "The destruction of books. The inundation of books. Books being overtaken by a flood. It makes me think of the books at the library of Alexandria, although those were destroyed by fire. Here they drown. I don't know what's worse."

"Burning's worse," I said emphatically. "Its more violent. It's more traumatic. But the flooding of books is more insidious. You think the books might still be saved, but they're also just as gone. They might as well be ash."

We began walking again. Night had fully fallen and an ocean breeze wafted its warm air currents redolent of the sea. The sea was but a few miles in either longitudinal direction. I was glad my library was on the mainland, in South Miami, on the Coastal Atlantic Ridge, seventeen feet above sea level. I wondered if those few feet would make enough of a difference, when the waters came.

Chapter 4

I began to do research on the changes expected due to the warming of the earth.

As a direct cause of our wanton implementation of fossil fuels, temperatures are projected to rise, first at a steady clip, then exponentially. The polar ice caps, the world's glaciers, all the permafrost no longer so permanent, are melting, adding to the volume of the oceans and releasing even more trapped carbon dioxide and methane, hastening the rise in temperature at an even faster pace. To be appended to this cycle is the equation that governs the effect of temperature on liquid: the warmer the liquid gets, the more it expands. I quickly gathered that our elevation of seventeen feet would only buy my neighbors and me a couple of decades before our houses, too, would succumb to the ineluctable ingress of water. Maybe for a few years, those who settled on the Coastal Atlantic Ridge will enjoy waterfront properties. But then the inevitable tide will take us all.

Funny, for the moment, nobody is panicking. Nobody is packing.

Thank God my library is on the second floor.

Still, the added humidity would add to the exertion of the air conditioning units and dehumidifier. But wait! Would we even have electricity? I mean, there's electricity in Venice. If they could do it there, we can do it here.

After Andrew, the big hurricane of 1993 (I was in a different house back then), we were without electricity for over two weeks. The humidity slid in and started to do its dirty deeds on the books. The leather-bounds started to stick together. I separated them to have air circulate all around them. I had to remove books from the shelves as the tomes swelled. The second week, the mold crept in and began to streak the leather-bounds with fuzzy growths. Every other day I had to wipe the books clean with a barely damp cloth and then rub them with a dry one. As soon as the power came back on I allowed the dehumidifier to function day and night for a week, until the humidity read 50% again. We're so humid in South Florida that at times our indoor humidity reads 90%, even when it's not raining.

Once we have standing water all around us, what will happen to our books? They'll swell up like sponges, they'll grow beards of mold, they'll start to curve and buckle, they'll adhere to each other, deformed and enlarged in crooked rows of softened covers. Once they're submerged, however, there will be no saving them. They'll be lost to us forever.

I will have to send my more important books to the Svalbard Vault, on the Norwegian island of Spitsbergen, although I hear only seeds are stored there. They'll have to open up a new cavern where books can be held. But they'll have to be encased in an impermeable shield so the ice crystals won't penetrate into the pages.

Iris had succeeded in alarming me. The following month, with the coming of the King tide, my anxiety hit a new high. My seventeen-foot buffer did nothing to quell my malaise. A visit to Miami Beach heightened my disquiet. Water sloshed onto many roads, sidewalks disappeared, water came up manholes, docks were submerged.

George was waiting for me in front of his apartment building. He wore shorts and flip-flops, ready to traverse the soggy terrain. I on the other hand made the mistake of wearing regular shoes and jeans. The water mark came up mid-ankle.

We found Iris seated on the edge of a concrete planter in the middle of Lincoln Road Mall. This tourist extravaganza is a mile long and open to the elements, attracting specimens of humanity that implement the Surrealists's decree that the weird, the unorthodox and the disquieting should all be juxtaposed with the normal and the humdrum. This evening, the Mall was dry and teeming with humanity. The restaurants were full and there were long lines of people waiting to go in. There was even a long line of patrons waiting outside of Books and Books, each with a book in her hand. I gathered there was a book signing.

We walked up to Iris. The Knife materialized from nowhere. We went through our usual exchange, charitable donations from George and me to Iris; money transfer from Iris to The Knife; poems released to George and me.

I held my bit of paper in front of me and said to Iris, "I'd like to publish these, Iris. I want to publish a book of your poetry as soon as possible. May I have your permission to collect these poems and organize them and make a book out of them?"

Iris answered in English that had an incongruous New York City accent.

"This writing is not mine. I give it to the people to whom it belongs. Not that they believe what is written, or even understand it, but each piece has been written for them in mind. It is Kronos who dictates the writing to me, and he knows the people I shall run across on any given day."

She reached out and touched the slip of paper she had just given me.

"I see what you are doing," she continued. "You are making a brave attempt to try to bring order to a chaotic thing. These random bits of writing speak of many things, for many people, because that is life. Life is chaos. Humans are the only beings who are afraid of chaos. They try most of their lives, wasting much of their life, in the attempt to bring order to the chaos. You yourself will succeed in your endeavor. You separate and divide, you classify and you organize, you line them up, all these harbingers that Kronos dictates to me. You will make chapters of them, write a foreword, annotate and justify the text. This I see. I see all of it. Your book will be beautiful, people will like it. There will be a book signing, although not there."

She pointed to the queue outside the Books and Books.

"People will buy it, you will sign it—"

"You'll sign it, too!" I interjected.

"I will write a new forecast for each person, alerting them to a piece of their fate. But in the end, no one will take heed. They'll all take the book home, read it, enjoy it, leave it on their kitchen table or by their bed, or slip it between other books on a shelf. And I'll be able to follow each and every one of those books in each and every house and see how the water overtakes them, flows over them, engulfs them. I'll see some of them float for a while, until they become trapped under a piece of furniture or under the ceiling. Soon they all sink, among the debris of your ordered lives, the jetsam of your carelessness, the clutter of your apathy. Your well-ordered lives will prove to be a thin veneer, a pathetic attempt to bring order to chaos. The universe knows no order. You believe that just because you think you understand some of the movements of the heavens that the universe will lay down for you. It's pitiable, really. It's like understanding the movement of the asteroid as it works its way through your local solar system headed straight for you. 'Ah, we understand!' you all cry out before it shatters you to smithereens. It will be the same when the water comes. Only at the end will you cry out, 'Ah, we understand!' before the water closes on your houses. The unfortunate will congregate on the top floors of your highest skyscrapers, there to wait out an inevitable and lonely death. The monstrosities that await them are such that they will realize it would have been better to be among the first to drown. After consuming their pets and each other, what else will they have to feed their tenacity to cling to life? Life is determined, but it is nothing next to the chaos of the universe. Those last ones will have enough time to wonder if humanity's tampering with the Earth had anything to do with their destruction. Of course it did! But what will it matter once everybody's gone? Too late. Way too late. Even now, it's way too late."

I wished we were anywhere but on the median strip of Lincoln Road Mall, surrounded by hundreds of people, each person or group walking past the others on their individual trajectory. There were a thousand vectors, with arrows of movement, crisscrossing, intermingling, intersecting their multitudinous paths. White mice scurrying in a laboratory labyrinth seemed less chaotic, less pathetic.

The future as predicted by Iris was depressing as hell. I garnered my courage and asked her the question that had been burning inside my head ever since I'd started reading her poems.

"Is it really too late? If we stopped using fossil fuels cold turkey, if we switched to renewable energy sources, if we—"

My voice trailed off as I noticed Iris's eyes focusing directly into mine. This is the first time she had ever done that.

"Knowing humanity like you do—don't shrug, you're a novelist, therefore you know what is in men's hearts—do you really think that those people who make a profit from fossil fuels, and the other people who invest in them, do you really think that they will desist in the face of overwhelming evidence? You will have to pry the money from their cold, stiff hands before that will happen. Look at you, so conscientious, so pure-hearted. You own stocks, you own mutual funds. Have you taken a close look at what's in them? You should divest yourself of such investments before you throw the first stone, don't you think? Ah, you think it's all complicated, that it would take time. But so long as the market value of your treasures keeps going up and up, you don't want to take a close look. You yourself are part of the problem. You may congratulate yourself for driving a hybrid, but half the time you're using petrol. And even if you have a fully electric car, where do you think electricity comes from? You think electrons are free for the taking from the air? Every one of you who drives a car is a straw on the camel's back. But no individual straw wants to take responsibility for adding to the weight. After all, you're just a straw. But when the camel's back breaks, all of your cars, guzzlers, hybrids and electric, will provide the structure for all the new coral reefs of the world. They will provide great hiding spaces for sea creatures, their leather interiors will even feed some of them. Humanity thinks that global warming will cause the sea to rise little by little, increment by increment, that you will have time to move all your belongings to the second floor, have time to move your books to Orlando. That is not how it will be. When Nature has had enough, she will put up a hand, and this will be enough to unleash the currents. The Gulf Stream will reverse, the waters will come down from the Great Lakes and up the Mississippi from New Orleans and meet in New Madrid, the center of a new inland sea. The same thing will happen up the Amazon and the Nile and the Ganges and the Danube and the Yellow, and great new lakes will be formed that will dwarf the Great Lakes. You here on the coast, of course, will be history. Your books will be as surprised as you are when the water comes."

Iris closed her eyes the better to see. "Water is the baptism of the new Earth, to cleanse herself, rid herself of all the impurities, the contamination, the chemicals, the plastics, the hydrofluorocarbons that long have been the product of mankind's progress."

Iris's eyes remained closed as she shifted her weight as if to see the heavens.

"Hearken, then," she intoned, with a deeper, authoritarian voice, "hearken to how She reacts to all that man hath wrought; despair at the sight, for he hath wrought his own death."

It was as if she had grown. Her voice resounded in the mall that was like a canyon, and her voice echoed back to us from the façades of the stores and restaurants. Passersby turned and stared. George, The Knife and I could only stand there and look at her in silence and in awe.

∞

Time and oblivion are the same: your artifacts will outlast you
    by mere centuries, a millennia or two.
After that, nothing. Your marvels removed by a renewal
    of the earth whose mantle never ceases to move;
Life will continue without you, even better without you,
    and the echoes of your lament will die in the wind.

∞

Chapter 5

I was teaching on the morning that George texted me with bad news about Iris.

"Iris is in the hospital," it said. "Call me."

I sent my French students to do their lab work and I rushed to my car, calling George as I ran.

"What happened?" I asked.

"She's okay, but she's been beaten up."

I thought it was kids who had beaten her up, using the homeless for sport and amusement, honing their violence on the hapless.

I was wrong. When I met George at the hospital, he told me that she had been stoned by a hysterical group of Christian proselytizers.

One of her eyes was swollen shut when I walked into the room. The other was covered by bandages around her head. There were nicks and bumps on her face, including a pretty big gash on her chin that had been closed with sutures.

"How's she doing?" I asked George.

The sound of my voice made her open her eye as much as she could.

"*¡No soy bruja!*" she cried out. "*¡No soy bruja!*"

I looked at George. "What the...!"

He nodded, as surprised as I was. He was closest to her and placed a comforting hand on her shoulder.

"It's okay," he said in Spanish. "You're safe here. Nobody will harm you here."

She saw who was there in the room with her and recognized us. She seemed to calm down, but she said one more time, "*¡No soy bruja!*" before her eye closed again.

I whispered to George, "Why is she saying that she's not a witch?"

"I suppose the Christian people who attacked her went into a fury and called her a witch. I mean, these people think agnostics are Satanists. It happened in front of the Bank of America on Collins. The group, you know, the ones that carry bibles and hound and pester people to death and don't give up till you run away, they began picking up garden stones by the drive-in lanes to fling them at her. The drive-in teller called the police, but not before Iris had been hurt badly. I found out about it because The Knife called me."

"Where is The Knife now?"

"He's in his own room, down the hall. He was hurt as well. Not as badly, but these people aimed for their heads. They seemed to know what they were doing."

"Well, they know all about stoning, don't they? They read about it every day. Time to put it into practice. To them, Iris is a witch. She predicts the future. She tells people their destiny."

"Yeah, and The Knife looks like the perfect witch consort, dark and wiry. Only the black cat was missing."

"What are the doctors saying?"

"That she'll be all right. They want her to stay overnight for observation, same as The Knife."

"Où est-il?" she asked.

I answered in the same language. "He's also here at the hospital, in a different room."

"Est-ce qu'il va bien?" she asked of him.

"Yes, he's doing okay."

"He defended me. He threw his body over mine."

"We should call him The Shield *(Le Bouclier)*, then," I said, trying to make light, but Iris didn't even smile. George didn't understand French.

"They were calling me a witch *(une sorcière)*."

"Those people don't understand. They hate anybody who

differs from them. They even hate other Christians."

"*Ich bin müde,*" she said next, turning to German.

My German isn't the best, but I understood that she was tired. "*Wollen Sie alleine sein?*" I asked her. Do you want to be alone? "*Ja, bitte. Ich möchte schlafen.*" Yes, please. I'd like to sleep.

I translated to George and we both walked out. In the hallway, we spoke about how we could help Iris after she was released from the hospital.

"I have an extra room in my apartment. It has a day bed in it."

I looked at George with admiration. He was willing to put Iris up at his place. Not wishing to be outdone in generosity, I replied, "So do I, as a matter of fact." Then I could have bitten my tongue as I anticipated the problems of having Iris staying with me.

"She won't stay at your place."

"Oh, no? Why not?"

"Because she won't leave the island. She goes as far as the Venetian Causeway, but only half way. It's like there's a barrier for her."

I was relieved, but I said, "Oh, well. What a shame. She'll stay at your place."

"Only if she wants to. She can be very opinionated, you know."

"You might have The Knife coming by every day."

"I don't mind. He doesn't bother me. He is rather strange."

"Yet he did protect her. According to what she said."

"No, I didn't gather that. I didn't understand."

"Ah, sorry. She said that he had shielded her body with his when they were pelting her with rocks. That was very courageous of him."

"Yes, it was."

We stopped by his room and peeped in, but the bathroom door was open and obstructed the view of the bed. We heard a low droning. Curious, we walked in slowly.

The Knife was in bed, also with a bandaged head, also with cuts and bruises about the face. He was humming a melody at a very low pitch. When he saw us peek around the door he smiled and said in English, "Come in! Come in!"

"Are you okay?" asked George.

"I okay, I okay," he answered. "Pain, much pain," he intoned, patting his head, then his shoulders, then sending a hand to his lower back.

"What happened?" I asked.

The Knife switched to French, which I translated to George. "What happened? I'll tell you what happened. Iris walked up to the people in white uniforms and expected them to act like normal, sane people. After they refused to give her money, they shouted to her in Spanish to get a job. Of course, she didn't speak to them, but she went up to one of them and gave her one of her papers. It was in Spanish because the woman understood the poem. She started yelling at Iris, calling her a witch. A witch from hell. *Une sorcière des Enfers.*"

The Knife raised his hands and shook them as if to describe the pandemonium that ensued.

" 'Stone her!' shouted one of them, picking up a rock. He threw it at her. Then the others ran to the rocks and threw them at her. I ran to Iris and told her to get down. Then I covered her with my body, but she is taller than I. It was hard covering her body all at once. Then the police came. The white-uniformed people scattered like flies. Cowards! Ugly people! When I raised myself off of Iris, I realized that she was unconscious. I thought maybe she was dead! But the ambulance came and the people revived her. One of the stones landed on her skull, right here. A little more force, and she could have died. But I was there with her, all the way!"

The Knife was not very big, but he had certainly shown a lot of courage that day.

He asked about Iris and we told him that she had been awake and feisty, but that she was feeling tired.

"I'll check on her later," he told us.

On the way out of the room, I saw a whiteboard on the wall, with the patient's name and the name of the nurse on call. Once out in the hallway, I chuckled.

"What is it?" asked George.

"You know, what we thought was The Knife's name?"

"What about it?"

"It's not The Knife." I hesitated for greater effect. "It's de Naïf. His name is Réginald de Naïf."

George didn't get it. He's a mathematician, not a linguist.

"His name means naive," I said. "He's no knife; he's naive."

"Well, whatever his name is, he certainly rose to the occasion today."

"That he did," I agreed. "That he certainly did."

After we left the hospital, we decided to visit the scene of the stoning. There were still rocks on the sidewalk. There was also a swarm of pieces of paper stuck in the bougainvillea in front of the bank. The plants were pruned into low shrubs and many of Iris's poems had been skewered by the spines. We carefully plucked them from their spikes and I put them in my pockets. I took them home and added them to my growing collection of Iris's poetry.

The following poem, translated from Spanish, is the one that I believe must have incited the first zealot Christian proselytizer to stone Iris. It was crumpled up into a tight ball when I found it. I almost didn't see it, it looked so much like one of the stones.

∞

No More Gods

Your time has also come to a sudden end.
No soliciting enemies to offend,
No driving back pagans, ejecting heathens,
You are out of time; there'll be no more seasons

For you to wander the wilderness, canvass
The neighborhood to thwart ungodly madness.
No Christ can help, no deus ex machina
In glorious descent like Zeus, Athena,

Or Thor, Buddha, Quetzalcoatl, even Ra:
They are mute, spent, impotent, and no more awe
Can ever rise from each degraded icon.

Kronos is the sole god left, the one who won:
The others kneel and bow, scrape and supplicate
For time to delay his sure and deadly rate.

∞

Chapter 6

*O*f Iris were truly a seer, why hadn't she predicted her attack and avoided it?

George and I couldn't figure out if she was a prophetess, a clairvoyant, or a visionary. Cassandra had been given the gift to see the future. But when she refused to give her body as recompense to the god Apollo, he punished her by having no one believe her. Cassandra had seen the destruction of Troy by the Greeks hiding inside a huge wooden horse, but the Trojans fell for the ruse anyway. She even saw her own death, but was powerless to prevent it.

Was Iris like one of the Sibyls at the Oracle of Delphi? Did she go into a trance and receive visions from an unknown source? Was she a new Nostradamus, writing cryptic verses to warn us of the Apocalypse? Was she like Swedenborg who could travel to other planets and learn the secrets of the universe? Was she a Wiccan, versed in the dark arts of divination and the divinity of Nature, which are one and the same? Was she a shaman or a sham?

I didn't care. I just wanted to publish her poetry. But was I guilty of trying to use her for my machinations, for my benefit, for my profit? I could easily justify it by telling myself that I wanted to find a broader audience for her auguries. If we had a new Nostradamus on our hands, wouldn't it profit society to know of her prophecies? And surely there was no harm in a prophet showing profit? In spite of her protestations that people wouldn't heed her warnings, we still had to try. We couldn't just give up.

Besides, I for one believed everything she said and wrote. I don't know how Iris had known that I owned mutual funds, but that made my hair stand on end. I had even asked George if he had told her. George had responded with his usual aplomb, "I didn't know you owned mutual funds. Iris just knows things. She knows things about the future. So if she knows something about your mutual funds in the future, she can follow them back to the present."

"Wow!" I said in admiration. "Maybe she can help me choose my mutual funds."

"She won't do that."

"Why not?"

"She won't tamper with anything having to do with gambling. I once asked her to tell me who would be the winner of a football game. She refused."

I called my portfolio manager and told him to sell everything that even appeared to have anything to do with chemicals, especially the gas companies. He was used to my eccentricities: years ago I had had him sell my stocks in tobacco companies and in manufacturers of weapons. I had vacillated about selling my stocks in the companies that made spirits, but I decided I liked vodka too much, and also absinthe.

Chapter 7

Today I received Iris's blessing to publish her book.

She even gave me the poem she wants to be first. It's one of her longest poems. Since it combines several of her favorite themes, I agree that it should be first. It should also be alone, in its own chapter. It left me disconsolate. I wonder if it will incite anyone to do anything.

∞

Fog and Water

Fog will fall and drag its prickly particles
        over town and country
Like damp gauze submerging even sound,
        Trees dripping in sweat.
Rivulets on glass and walls are but precursors
        to the swell and bulge of tide water
                the day after.

                What can we do,
You ask for the final time, your hands fluttering
        in the air.
The answer, so heavy and obvious,
        rushes in silently,
On little mouse feet,
        scurrying in from all directions,
                also up the toilets.

Where shall we go,
You ask with your cars useless
        on the driveway,
One in the garage which is the first to flood.
        Some of you start a trek
With courage born of despair,
        inland you go,

                                inland and inland.

                                How long do we have,
You ask as water laps at your feet,
        your ankles,
Your calves. You hold your children up high.
        The strength of water
Is a force of nature that none can defy.
        With water at your thigh

                                fatigue sets in.

                                How long do we have,
You repeat your question as you look
        for things to climb:
Stalled trucks, trees, electric posts, radio masts.
        But the water comes
And still it comes, swirling with a surface
        glistening in oil,

                                inevitable.

                                How did this come to be,
Is your final question, your hands fluttering
        in the air.
Your fate, too, was as inevitable as it was
        forewarned.
Now you tread the very water you set loose,
        as unaware

                                as ever.

Silence reigns.
The world asks no questions for it has
no curiosity.
Same as you were, blind, impervious to
the evidence everywhere:
Trees flowering early, birds migrating late,
caterpillars cocooning no more.
Glaciers melting.

Your time is gone.
No more questions, you are silenced
as you sink to the silt.
The fog leaves, the water stays
over new geography.
Ego next to water stands no chance.
A question floats unasked:
Is this justice?

The Earth blinks and shrugs.

∞

Chapter 8

The police got involved in Iris's attack.

Officers came to her hospital room and asked her a great deal of questions. George and I weren't there, but de Naïf was. He had been released from the hospital, but since he had nowhere to go, he hung around Iris's room. I suppose he also took his loyalty and duty to protect her seriously.

The Christian zealots were nowhere to be found. The cowards had retreated to their lair and the police had no idea where to start looking for them. The bank's outside cameras had caught part of the action, but the Christians were all wearing caps that sported the words, "JESUS IS COMING!" in bold, red letters. The caps obscured most of their faces.

I had a hunch as to where these Christians could be found. I've had a sneaking suspicion that they are amassing very far west in our county, way beyond Krome Avenue, halfway into the Everglades. There they've been building massive churches and prayer halls to their heart's content, bothered by no one since there's nobody there. But I suppose that the Miami Beach police can't be bothered to go searching so far out of their jurisdiction. In the end, the cops didn't do much. The victims were pummeled and lacerated, but there were no broken bones and no lasting injuries. Iris was told sternly not to accost any more passersby. She gave no promises; the cops didn't ask for any. Instead, she gave each officer a gift of her poetry. I was vexed that I would never get to see any of those poems.

I accompanied George to the hospital the day Iris was released. We took her to George's flat and made her comfortable in the second room which George uses as a study. I could tell that he had removed cartons of books and a hoard of bric-a-brac from the room because, for once, it looked stark. About the only personal item he had left on the only table of the room was his tabletop computer. He would be able to use his laptop and a myriad of other electronic gizmos that seemed to proliferate in the remaining rooms: ipods, ipads, iwatches, istuff, some with girls' names, Siri, Alexa, Cortana, that I knew nothing of. George is so fully plugged into the state-of-the-art world that I think he himself must recharge his batteries by plugging himself into the wall. He talks to his virtual girlbots as if they were his friends, although many times he complains that they should be boybots. In any case, those bots give the illusion that they're thinking creatures but they've just been fed a lot of information about where to get pizza delivered and who built the first bathyscaphe.

Iris went into George's study with no qualms whatsoever. She saw the bed, converted from a sofa, and went to it automatically and sat down on its edge. She said nothing, but her smile meant that she was probably looking forward to sleeping on a real bed. Well, as real as it can be, since originally it was a sofa.

Here is one of the poems written in George's apartment:

∞

Had we evolved quickly enough
    we should have had nostrils atop our head,
Sinuous bodies to move through water,
    flippers and fins and no hair,
Webbed fingers but no toes.
    Of what use are toes when deep in water;
Lungs, too, are a waste, for we should have grown
    gills.

∞

Chapter 9

A few days later it was the weekend.

I came by to visit George and Iris, and found de Naïf there as well. George opened the front door for me. As I walked into the living room, Iris came out of her boudoir; de Naïf came out of George's bedroom, wearing a bathrobe and slippers.

A fleeting look of sheepishness crossed George's face before he recovered and offered me coffee.

"Yes, please. Coffee is the elixir of life!" I said flamboyantly, to dispel his feeling of discomfiture.

But I forgot that George was Cuban. He brought out coffee in these tiny plastic cups, the liquid swirling in them thick as molasses. You really couldn't sip this coffee. It was more like shots. I preferred to linger over my coffee, served in big Gien cups with images of the Little Prince on them and on the saucers.

We all sat around George's round table next to the kitchen. Iris still had bluish marks on her face and I asked her and de Naïf how they were feeling.

"Much better," answered de Naïf. "Much better. Pain gone away. Stitches on Iris's head coming out soon."

I looked at the bandage still on Iris's head, above her right eye and a bit towards her temple.

I smiled at her. "I'm glad," I said. "I hope you never approach those people again."

"She is not approach," offered de Naïf. "She says she don't see them now. In the future, I mean. They not part of the future now. They probably not even on the Beach no more. The police still looking for them. The police also after Iris."

"What? What do you mean?"

It was George who explained next. "The police have warned Iris not to approach this Christian group. Of course, they don't understand when she says that they have been eliminated. That created quite a ruckus."

"Eliminated? Eliminated?" I asked, my hand at my throat.

"See? They had pretty much the same reaction," said George. "What Iris meant was that the Christians have been eliminated from her future. Apparently they've gone into hiding in whatever hole they hide in, and have not been seen on the Beach at all. I mean, the police have images of them. They should be able to identify them and have them all arrested. But the cops still want to make life difficult for Iris, however. As if it had all been her fault."

"Not my fault," exclaimed Iris.

"We know it's not your fault," said George. "You did nothing wrong. Your First Amendment rights are fully protected. You can hand out as many prognostications as you wish. Nobody can stop you. Moreover, I don't think anybody *can* stop you."

George turned to me and explained, "She went out last night. Just for a few hours. She said that there were people she was going to meet who absolutely needed her slips of paper. It was a matter of life or death, she said."

I looked at Iris. She sat in her chair as regal as a queen. Her beautiful blue eyes shone with a sheen that made her whole look sparkle. She was vivacious, vibrant, vital.

"Iris." I cleared my throat. "I wish to tell you something. De Naïf is wonderful and all, but he is not enough to protect you."

"I am enough—" de Naïf started to protest.

"No, you are not. You're great, but Iris needs all our help. I am also here to help. George, too. Moreover, I have a car. I can take you to where you're going to meet your… your…"

I didn't know what to call the people who were the recipients of her little slips of paper. Her customers? Her legatees? Her beneficiaries?

"My souls," she finished for me.

"Your… souls," I repeated. "You will be protected, and you will still be able to meet with your souls. Perhaps you will even be able to meet them faster," I offered with hopes that she would accept my chivalrous proposition.

She looked at me, not with the gratitude I would have desired, but rather with the look of appraisal of someone bargaining for a used car.

"Yes," she said. "I think it could work."

She said "wohk" with a definite English accent.

I imitated it. "By Jove," I said. "I think it could veddy well wohk."

George laughed. Neither Iris nor de Naïf did.

I went back to my regular accent. "It could work, I think."

Chapter 10

That very same evening I returned at six, an hour before sunset.

Everybody trooped into my car.

"Where are we going first?" I asked.

Iris was the one who answered. "To the park. By the pool."

She meant Flamingo Park, by 12th Street.

"Some of your souls will be there to meet you?"

"They don't know they will meet me. They will be just passing by. I am going to intercede on their behalf."

"Intercede?" I questioned. "Intercede for whom?"

"For Kronos," was her immediate response.

When I hesitated, George, who had gone into the back seat with de Naïf, spoke up. "Kronos, the Titan, Lord of Time. It is he who is responsible for the destiny of us all."

I thought for a minute. "You mean to tell me, Iris, that when you intercede for your souls, there is a chance that they will be able to change their destiny?"

"Yes," Iris answered. "Destiny is fluid. Destiny is not stone."

"But how do you know the people with whom you are supposed to cross paths?"

"In my mind I see a flame. The flame flickers in many directions. Inside the flame as it flashes brighter, I see people, and I see them at the spot where they will be. I simply go to them and meet them. I know they will be there. I know who they are, and, part of the information that the flame gives to me, is the knowledge of their destiny, especially the end of their existence on earth. I know where they will be when they die. I know what they will be doing when they die. I know if they will be with others, and if those others will accompany them in death, or not. If their death can be modulated by a simple change in their present, then Kronos allows me to tell them. Lately, this procedure has been quickening, for many people are going to die soon, and together, for the same reason. I reach out to individual souls, especially those who look after others, such as children or other relatives. If I can save one such soul, I save many who would die chronologically in proximity. Time is running out."

I felt a chill inside of me.

By this time we were on Michigan Ave, driving south. My heart was so despondent over what I had just heard I could barely steer my car. For the next few blocks my right foot wasn't even on the accelerator; it was hovering over the brake pedal. At the intersection on 13th Street, I had to stop at a red light. I felt better not moving.

I needed to know something right away. "But, Iris… But, Iris… Do these people… Do they believe you? Do they believe what you write on the slips of paper?"

"That is not my affair," she answered, with a look of preternatural calm about her, as if nothing of the present could unnerve her. "I warn. If people heed the warning, then my work is done. Some people crumple up the papers and throw them to the gutters and keep on walking. Those people I cannot reach. But some people do read my poems. All it takes is a glance. Some understand. Some identify the truth in the writing. They identify themselves in the writing. They recognize that I know about them, and that I describe things nobody else could know. They read, and they trust. That is all I can ask for."

"I wonder if any of them do anything about it… about what you write, I mean."

"That is something else I cannot worry about. After they leave me, they are away from my attention. Kronos does not let me see them anymore. I won't meet them again. Very few people keep coming back into my vision. You, for instance. You're very persistent."

We were approaching the area of the park where the pool and the basketball courts were.

"So, you keep seeing me in your visions?"

"My visions?"

"Yes. Don't you have visions?"

"Not my visions. My vision. You make it seem as though I see hallucinations, delusions. No, mine is vision. Just like your vision as you move about, clear, concise, focused. That is mine. Only it's in the future. I see every particle, I see every movement, as if it were happening in front of me now. Only I know—I have ascertained—that what I see is in the future."

"How far into the future?"

"That I don't know. Kronos has no way of telling me when it will be. I can figure out where it will be. I can look out of a window, see around me. I've traveled so much around this earth, I usually can identify the place. But the time of what I witness, only if there is a calendar lying around, or a computer screen on, can I tell. When I see what I see, I cannot interact with the people, or with the things in my vision. I cannot go to a computer screen and click on the date. I cannot talk to the people. I just see them during an important part of their future. That is what I write about. I write about what Kronos allows me to see."

"Have you seen Kronos?"

"Of course, he is everywhere."

"What do you mean, everywhere?"

"Kronos is everywhere around us. He is with us night and day. He makes night and day. He cannot be avoided. He suffuses our every move, our every thought, our every dream. If we reminisce, if we plan, if we move from one space to the next, he is with us. We carry him inside of us, he accompanies us outside of us, we are forever beholden to him. When it is our time to separate ourselves from him, we crumble into dust."

"Why do you call him a him?"

"Purely for the sake of convenience. In Latin-based languages he is masculine: *le temps, el tiempo, il tempo;* but in German, she's feminine: *die Zeit.* In Russian, it's neuter, *время.* Call Kronos what you will, use whatever pronouns you want, whatever names you feel comfortable with. It doesn't change his, her, its character at all. He, She, It keeps being Time, as in *Tempus fugit,* and we owe him, her, it our life, our very existence, our moments moving about on this earth, and when we part from him, her, it… we die."

"Is that how it works?" I asked, pulling into a parking space.

"That is how it works," she replied.

As soon as the car had stopped moving, she collected all her bags and opened the car door. But she hesitated and looked back at me.

"You at least try," she said to me.

"I try?"

"Yes, you try to establish your existence after you die."

"I do?"

"In your writing. Writing is good to extend your life after your life is over. People in the future will be reading you, thus devising an existence after your physical self is gone."

"You mean?" I looked right into Iris's eyes. "You mean, I will endure?"

Iris didn't smile at me, for she never smiled, but I could tell that a sentiment of tenderness settled on her expression.

"Yes," she said quietly. "You will endure."

Then she said something that brought the chill back into my heart.

"For as long as your books will physically endure."

With that, she was out of the car, with de Naïf and George following her. I had to run a bit to catch up to them.

She had let me see the poems that she was going to distribute that evening. I had time to transcribe them. Here is one of them:

∞

To a lady walking her dog on 9th and Lenox:

The dress you put on your dear Lizzy
clings to her fur and bogs her down
but your dead hand holds on to her leash

she drowns with you
        though you won't know her sacrifice

Let her go let her free no clothes or leash
she'll stay with you until that final day

you can't be saved but know that she can
if only you choose to let her go.

∞

After the ninth poem, Iris had no more to disseminate. We slowly walked back to the car. I drove them home in silence.

Chapter 11

I couldn't help wondering why some people do nothing in the face of peril.

Many people freeze when threatened. Psychologically explained, it's the fight or flight syndrome, but freeze is another option that nature has construed for living organisms to outsmart their predators.

I remember once a neighbor kid giving me a wild hare he had caught in the Everglades. He knew I had a rabbit so I suppose he thought I'd like to have a hare as well. We released the hare in one of my bathrooms. As soon as we opened its cage it ran out but then froze. Between the white toilet and the white sink, with white tile behind both, the brown hare stood stock still, following its instinct that this behavior would save it from predators. I remember feeling sorry for it because in this artificial environment he stood out against the white background, and its immobility would make it easier to grab.

Such are the stories of victims who go down with a sinking ship, who don't leave a burning building, who don't react to the imminent danger which threatens their very lives. Perhaps their instinct is an attempt to have destiny pass them by and leave them alone, but the boat is sinking, the building burning, the situation worsening. It does them no good. I think, rather, that they lose the ability to think. No power of reasoning reaches their cerebellum as deeper down, in their medulla oblongata, they surrender to a more ancient response and become paralyzed, to their own detriment. So many people drown when their car falls into a canal; they forget to undo their seatbelts.

But what is the excuse for otherwise intelligent people who, when faced with danger that is not as immediate, still fail to act? The reasons, as they say, are legion.

First of all, it *is* easier to do nothing. Go with the flow. Until the flow gets you.

Second, people are loath to leave their homes. Real estate being what it is, even though they know that they will be underwater, they still don't want to leave. Some need to see the water lapping at their front stoop before they make a decision to act. Others need to see the water level rise in their living rooms. Others will drown in their attics.

I suppose people are optimists and don't think that the situation will ever get that bad. Think of the frog that will jump right out if you throw it into a pot of boiling water. But if you place it in comfortably warm water and turn up the heat in slow increments, you end up with frog soup.

There are those who think that bad things visit only other people, evil people, people who are different, foreign people, weird people, queer people. They have faith in their god and in the son of their god and their holy ghost and their virgin and their saints and their myriad of other intercessors who will save them, who at the last minute will part the sea, part the lava, part the lahar, part the tsunami and leave them high and dry, exposed only to his/their love in the sun while the others float in the waves or burn in the cinders. Like the idiots who "thank the lord" for having saved them from the twister, willfully ignoring the fact that it was the lord who sent it to them in the first place. Meantime, their neighbors rot under their demolished houses.

People are besotted with their remote controls. They watch the twister on T.V. instead of going outside to watch it. That is, until the power goes out. Then they stew in the heat without air conditioning, bored with the reality of their lives.

Then, for a small percentage of the people, there is the dubious pleasure of anticipating a catastrophe, though they keep it a secret. Knowing the dangers of staying put, inhabitants of the coast are known to gang up in "hurricane parties" to enjoy the thrill of the risk, the heart-thumping sound of the screaming winds, the menacing crash of thunderous waves against the pilings. Perhaps those who wait for floods also wish to have their pulse quicken, their emotions rise. We think of ourselves as safe; danger beckons to us in varying intensity.

I for one have sold my farm in the Redlands; the swamp will be wanting to take that back any day now. I live on the Coastal Atlantic Ridge, hoping that that will be enough. My house in South Miami is seventeen feet above sea level. If that isn't enough, Florida will be inundated up to Orlando.

Chapter 12

*I*ris surprised us all.

She left George's apartment to go live on the streets again. De Naïf stayed with George, having grown comfortable living in a house where creature comforts are forthcoming, where food and beverages come in regularly-spaced deliveries, air conditioning hums incessantly, and the mattress in the bedroom and the sofa in the living room are as soft as clouds. I should perhaps be a little bit less of a cynic: de Naïf might in fact be in love with George who is, after all, lovable. George has no faults that I can see and perhaps he has qualities that I cannot see.

But now Iris was roaming the streets again, this time without protection. Not that de Naïf was ever a perfect bodyguard, but he could, at least—in theory—run to get help. George and I worry about Iris, especially when she refuses to tell us in advance where she plans to sleep.

"I need my freedom," she said in Spanish. *"Necesito mi libertad.* Staying at George's was disturbing my communications with Kronos."

I observed that her Spanish had a definitive Argentine accent. I thought it funny as I had just met an Argentine national at an art gallery just two days previously.

"But you said Kronos is everywhere," I told her.

"Yes, but I need to be away from walls. I cannot be inside walls. They diffuse the message. I need to be outside, free to feel the breeze, to see the sky, to smell the sea, to have nothing between me and Kronos."

Perhaps she saw the concern and the worry on my face. She added, "I appreciate what you and George offer me, safety and protection. But I cannot accept. I need to be free, without restrictions, in touch with the earth and with Kronos who runs the earth and everybody on it."

"Well, can we at least give you a cell phone?" I asked with ardent hope.

She stopped to think. What would Kronos think of her having a phone?

"I suppose that would be all right. Kronos communicates through air waves and photons of light. I can communicate through air waves as well."

"In case of an emergency," I added. "That way, you can call us if you're in any danger, or when you're lonely and need to hear a friendly voice."

Iris smiled. She smiled! For the first time, I saw her smile.

"I'm never lonely," she said, her smile waning. "Kronos is all I ever need, for he allows me to see the people I loved but who are now dead. He also allows me to see what they've become, now in the present, and who they'll be in the future. People I knew come to me night and day, they're always with me. Then the vision I have of strangers keeps me busy, as does the writing of my testament to them."

"Will you still show me your testament writing, so I can continue to collect material for your book?"

"Yes, if Kronos allows. We'll have to meet in the mornings, before I go out on my walks. We shall speak on the phone so you can find out where I am. But remember, I do take a break in the afternoon for lunch."

It was my turn to smile. "Of course, you do. I imagine even Kronos must sometimes take a rest."

Iris took offense. "Of course, he doesn't. Kronos never sleeps, never rests, never hesitates or delays. His energy is constant, his mastery of the universe unrelenting."

"Even at the speed of light?" I asked, to throw some physics in.
"That's when he's at his most energetic," she explained.

I gave her the phone, showed her how simple it was to use, and stored my number in the memory along with George's. Then she wandered away. I wished I could follow her and keep her safe, but I had my own life to live, my own people to love, my own stories to write.

Chapter 13

$\mathcal{I}$t was time to start editing Iris's book.

My partner, Clara Estrella, said we had more than enough material for a poetry book of at least 125 poems. This would be a hell of a lot more than most poetry books. If we included illustrations of Iris, we had easily up to 150 or 160 pages, which for a book of poetry, is quite lengthy.

The organization of the book would be done by the themes we could identify in Iris's poetry. There were, of course, the poems whose main subject was time. There were so many of those we probably wouldn't be able to include them all. Then there were those based on apocalyptic motifs, especially inundation. The Flood was everywhere, as was the baptism of the earth, like a renewal—a rebirth—of the planet, only without humans. Closely following would be those poems that served to blame humankind for the apocalypse. Then there were the avatar poems, those that spoke of the transmigration of the souls, and of the love that sometimes unites them. Finally were the poems that spoke of man's complacency, of how foolish he is and so astonishingly unaware of his impending demise on earth.

We had enough for a book, I agreed. Clara and I brought in our two copy editors, our graphic designer, and our illustrator for a meeting on a Wednesday afternoon. That Wednesday morning, Iris gave me a clutch of papers for me to keep, not just to transcribe.

"They're for your troop," she said.

"My troop?"

"Yes! Your helpers. Those who will help you with your book."

I had said nothing to Iris about our meeting. Not even George knew about it. By this time, of course, I was used to Iris finding out about things she couldn't possibly have known.

"Except that it's *your* book, Iris. We're working on *your* book."

She waved my statement away breezily. "It seems that you're the one interested in publishing it. I prefer to continue doing it my way, one soul at a time. So here, take these. They're for the girl with the dimples on her cheeks (I recognized that person as Clara); the girl with the white birthmark in her hair (Maria); the boy with the hair in front of his eyes (Rick); the tall, thin boy (Steve); the boy who speaks Spanish with an Argentine accent (Rogelio, our new illustrator); and the boy who comes to the meeting late (I didn't know who this was)."

I decided that I wouldn't read these bits of Iris's testament, nor transcribe them. They were personal. At the meeting, I distributed them among our staff. I sat there, observing them, as they read their bits. They were silent and, I could tell, unnerved. From that day forward, they treated this project with deference and with awe. They were converts to the cause.

It turned out that the boy who came to the meeting late was the one who delivered lunch to us.

Chapter 14

This is the only piece of writing from Iris that was not written in poetry. She left it in George's apartment, on a piece of paper rolled into a tube and stuck into a can of chocolate pirouettes where it really didn't blend. For a long time it smelled of chocolate.

Tempus fugit. Extempore. Temporal. Tempest. Temple. Temple, house of worship. Temple, side of the head. Apparently those two meanings of the word have nothing to do with time but with tension. Old English *tempel*, from Latin *templum*, for space stretched out to make a sacred area. The area on either side of the forehead comes from Latin *tempora*, plural of *tempus*, the thin stretch of skin between eye and ear. And stretching makes for tension.

Either way, you have the same word, but very different meanings. Coincidence? A case could be made for the temples as entrances to the sacred area of the mind. Also, a similar case could be made for a temple being a weak spot that can be broken by the mere blow of a weapon. One must accept the fact that the mind makes for a weak terrain in which to tend to a god, or gods. Ha! There's another one! Tend. From the Old French *tendre*, to stretch, as in stretching out a hand. A tent is a tent because it is stretched. You move your hand towards the god you want to tend, to care for, look after. One must attend to a god, deal with it, take care of it, make sure it has received all the sacrifices it needs, all the prayers it demands. One attends to a god by paying attention to it. Giving heed to it. In French, attention implies a warning to an imminent danger. *Attention!* they yell when you are about to walk into traffic or drink one too many alcoholic beverages. There's tension there as well.

My point is that neither temple-house-of-worship or temple-side-of-forehead is derived from the Latin *tempus,* time. The place you worship, inside a building, inside your head, has nothing to do with time. Instead, both temples derive from tension, a stretching out, a stretching thin. A stretching of skin, a stretching of a place intended for worship. There we go again! Intend. From the Latin *intendere,* extend, direct, as in, directing attention to something for a particular purpose.

In the temple I tend to my gods, direct my attention to these gods whom I intend to adore and in so doing attend to their every wish. This calls for great tension because the gods are known to pull us in every direction, stretching us taut like the canvas of a tent, like the skin over our temples. It is difficult to know what they want of us. So we just impute to them our own desires. Our gods want us to smite our enemies. Our gods want us to believe in them out of faith. Our gods want us to ascertain how many angels can dance on the head of a pin.

Much time is wasted in all this effort to tend to our gods. Much effort, too.

We think that our time here on earth will stretch to infinity. We are so mistaken. Kronos not only limits our time, but he has cast all of creation into an everlasting process of change. Our ancestors went through myriads of permutations before arriving at us. We ourselves are in the middle of fluctuation, alteration, transformation, adaptation. We cannot be pinned down at any moment because we are in the process of evolution. We don't stand still, we can't even stop to be ourselves because we are always in the perpetual motion of change. Tomorrow we won't be what we are today, and we certainly aren't today what we were yesterday.

In order to survive, in order to pass through the barriers of time, we must evolve into something that can survive. Had we become beings less bellicose and less gullible, perhaps we could have succeeded. If we could develop gills and fins we could yet survive.

Yet, Kronos does not give us the time to adjust. We've received the lessons time and time again, but we never learn, despite all that time we've had to observe and study our earth, our environment, and the other creatures that share our planet. The knowledge was there, but we couldn't endure the lessons. The wisdom is still there, but our tension is too great for us to pay attention. We even refuse to pay attention to the immediate dangers we face. We decided eons ago that it was more important to tend to our gods, attend to their every whim, extend our hands to their effigies, and contend with our lot in life. After all, religion intends for us to curtail all progress; churches demand the status quo and make absolutely no room for the havoc that science has wrought. Religion even demands that you not believe in the perpetual change of all creation, in the constant transmutation of ourselves and of our place on earth. We have doomed ourselves in our attempt at perfect, sacred immobility in a world of perpetual fluctuation. Not only have we failed, we have secured our own incontrovertible demise.

We certainly deserve it.

Chapter 15

*I*ris staggered back to George's a few evenings later, scaring us all.

George, de Naïf and I were having dinner when we heard furious knocking at the door. When George opened the door, we saw Iris on her knees, slumped against the jamb. At first we thought she was drunk, but that wasn't the case. Her speech was not slurred as much as it was jerky, and heavily accented with German, but there was no scent of alcohol on her. She had never been known to drink and we were loath to conclude that this was her problem.

She wasn't unsteady on her feet, yet she kept swaying rhythmically as she walked into the living room, with our help. The strangest thing of all was that she kept asking us what day it was, and what time it was. I knew that she, as a friend of Kronos, had never worried before about the date or the time. She knew time immediately (without mediation of any kind), intimately, and intrinsically. Besides, she lived in the perpetual land of timelessness where one day could be exchanged with another, one hour with another. All she knew was the parade of people she would meet on that day, down to the exact place and the exact time.

"There is something wrong," she announced to us when we sat her down on the couch and arranged cushions all around her, fearing that she would fall.

"Why do you feel there is something wrong?" I asked her. I felt her forehead for fever and her pulse for strength.

"I had very few poems for my souls tonight. Just four. But Kronos didn't tell me that it was going to be my fault that he didn't give me more."

"Of course, it's not your fault," I told her. "You're not feeling well, that's all. You relax now."

George was on the phone, calling for an ambulance. De Naïf brought her a glass of water with trembling hands. She drank it in one draft.

I knelt in front of her, taking her hands in mine. "Don't worry," I told her. "None of this is your fault," I repeated.

I truly believed this; it wasn't her fault that Kronos had chosen her for such a difficult role in life, to hand out pieces of paper with people's destinies written on them.

"Sie verstehen nicht," she said, turning to German. "You don't understand."

Then she said something in German I truly didn't understand. "Switch to French," I told her. "Or English or Spanish."

She turned to French. *"Ma télésthésie n'est plus là. Je n'ai plus ma télésthésie."*

I still didn't understand. She was saying that she didn't have her, what? telesthesia? She didn't have her telesthesia any more.

"What is that?" I asked in French.

De Naïf answered for her, also in French. "It's her ability to know things at a distance, without using her eyes or ears, or even her brain. She knows things across physical space, but also across time space."

What the hell was de Naïf saying? There was a word for what Iris had that enabled her to know things about people?

Iris squeezed her eyes shut which forced two tears to simultaneously trickle down her cheeks.

"I'm bereft," she whispered, turning to English. "I'm alone, all alone, so alone."

"No, you're not alone," I informed her a bit harshly. After all, there we were, George, de Naïf and myself, surrounding her, comforting her, soothing her. "You have us. We are all here, your friends. We care for you. We won't let anything bad happen to you."

Iris opened her eyes. "But what about you? Who will care for you? Who is not going to let anything bad happen to you?"

Her tears continued to spill from her eyes. "It's coming soon, you see. My chronovision has begun to blur. It's because we're getting close to the end."

She said that with such deep sadness that my blood froze. Did Iris mean that she was finding it difficult to perceive the future because the end that she had foreseen was crowding into the present? Was the future running out for us?

How much time did we have, I wondered.

We heard the ambulance coming down West Avenue.

Iris said nothing more as she lay back on the sofa, her eyes tightly closed.

Chapter 16

The next day the doctor explained to us that Iris had experienced a TIA.

Transient Ischemic Attack, also known as a mini-stroke. The doctor explained that stress could have brought it on.

"Have you recently experienced a stressful environment?" she asked pensively.

"Yes," replied Iris in a mournful moan. "I was stoned."

The doctor thought about this and said, "Well, usually it's not a stressful experience to be stoned."

In spite of the situation, George and I laughed.

"No," I explained. "She was recently stoned, with rocks, by a bunch of Christians. Look, she still has scars on her temple and on her chin."

Looking incredulous, the doctor entoned with scientific rigor, "In that case, it is reasonable to theorize that a concussion could have been the culprit."

Seeing our worried faces, she offered us some good news.

"There should be no residual symptoms after a few days. But I wouldn't let her drive for a while."

We laughed. "Oh, she doesn't drive," I said. "But she does like to walk."

"If she feels like walking, let her. Just somebody accompany her all the time. The last thing we want now is for her to take a tumble."

"You see, Riri," said de Naïf. "You can't take a tumble. Doctor's orders. I go wif you again."

Iris smiled.

But when the medical people had gone and it was just us left in the room, Iris turned serious.

"This did not happen inside my brain," she told us in English with a British accent.

What?

George was closest to her and asked, "What do you mean by that?"

Iris pointed to her temple. "This did not happen inside my brain. My brain is fine. My mind is fine."

Then she turned to de Naïf, and to French.

"Ce sont les parasites, encore une fois."

"It's the parasites, once again," I whispered into George's ear.

De Naïf seemed to understand what she was saying, but I didn't. I got up from my chair and walked towards her bed.

She continued speaking in French with me. Here is the simultaneous translation I gave to George:

"It has happened before, though not too often. Sometimes there is a problem when I need to hear Kronos's voice. There have been a few times when his voice is cut off from me completely. But last night there was just a wee bit of a problem. His voice was faint, and the exertion it took to try to hear him gave me vertigo. I still heard enough to understand where I am supposed to meet my souls today, and I was able to write their poems without hesitation. But I wasn't supposed to be taken to the hospital. Now they don't want to let me go."

"Well, can you call on Kronos to have him help you sort this out?" I asked her.

Iris chuckled. "Kronos does not hear my voice. None of the gods ever hears the voices of us mortals on the earthly plane."

"Then, you can never clarify his messages to you? You can never ask him questions, ask him to explain, even to repeat, or to find out—"

"Kronos has no time for any of that. He tells me once, and once only: where to go, whom to meet, and give the soul his message."

"Kronos has no time…? But, Iris, isn't he the king of time? Can't he stop it, slow it down, back it up, tie it up into a pretzel?"

Iris laughed again. "The god of time has no time for us mortals. From the very beginning he condemned us to follow time in only one direction. He doesn't even want to show us how he can go back in time, repeat time, stop it for as long as he wants. Showing us how he can control time would give us bad ideas, bitter ideas, of visiting happy times, seeing our loved ones who have died, whom we miss very much, of standing still at the happiest moment of our lives. Since we are condemned to follow time in only one direction, the direction we call chronological, Kronos has granted us one possible way to cheat time, that of being told of one possible terrible event in the future so that we might strive to thwart it. He has given us one chance to avoid this terrible event, if only we care to listen."

"But now even you can't hear his voice."

"I can still hear it," she said forcefully, cupping a hand to her ear. "It is there, but faint, and the parasites keep getting stronger. It's hard… It's hard to hear what he says. But here is the proof that I heard enough yesterday, when his voice first began to grow faint. But now I cannot leave, unless you help me to leave."

I looked at George and de Naïf. I don't think any of us wanted to help her decamp from the hospital.

I had a better idea.

"Give those to me," I said, meaning the slips of prophesying poems. "You will tell me exactly where I need to be at exactly the right time, and describe the people I'm supposed to meet. I will be your surrogate. They won't know any better. They aren't expecting any one in particular. It might as well be me. I can do this for you. You trust me, don't you?"

"Yes, I trust you. But I don't trust you to keep quiet."

"What do you mean?"

"You must remain silent as you give out these slips of paper to their rightful souls. You are not allowed to say anything, explain anything, clarify anything. They must be allowed to read the message alone, with no help, no interpretation, no commentary."

"I can do that! I don't have to say anything. I promise. I won't say anything at all."

"You're a writer," Iris said to me. "You are loquacious; you can't help it. You were born to explain, to expound, and even if you have to keep something a secret for a few pages, it is still all accounted for in the end. With these pieces of paper, you must not give any reason whatsoever to the recipient. If they crumple up the paper in your presence and throw it at your feet, you cannot get it for them. It is their choice. You must let them react with complete autonomy. You cannot inveigle, you cannot attempt to persuade, you cannot act on them physically. You simply walk away to your next appointment."

"I understand, Iris. I do. And I'm not always a writer. Sometimes I'm an actor. I can act the way you have instructed. I will be the most indifferent, the most impassive emissary Kronos ever had. He will be so pleased with me that maybe he'll begin to communicate things directly to me!"

Iris laughed outright at this, with a merry look in her eyes I had never witnessed before.

"You may not always act as a writer, perhaps this is true, but you certainly have the hubris of one," was her remark to me.

That last statement I didn't translate to George. Instead, I told him, "Today I won't be a writer. Today, I shall be a soothsayer."

Yeah, I told myself, of course I'm a writer. But when necessary, I can certainly stick to a script.

Chapter 17

O was able to hand out the poems on that one day without a single problem.

I met all eight people at the right time and the right place, but soon I was to figure out why I wouldn't be able to repeat this action on the following day. Something of an all-encompassing nature came up and swept all of our plans away as if they were little pieces of paper in a violent gust.

---

*H*ere is one of the poems written for distribution by the narrator.

∞

Inconstant Time

(Given to a retired professor of physics, strolling in Flamingo Park, enjoying the sunset.)

> Such confidence in your step!
> Such competence in your eye!
> Newton, Einstein, Fermi, Hawking
> > prop you up and inflate you
> So your skin is taut and shiny
> > your backbone ramrod straight
> > > your head held high;
> > > > your gaze to the horizon
> > > > and beyond.
>
> It's all a house of cards
> > built on systems and funda-

mental units and mathema-
tical calcula-
tions far from ac-
curate.

Where you and your ancestors err,
    where the cracks appear,
    is in your apprehension of time.
Time is no constant
    and your attempts to measure it,
calibrate and tame it are in vain.
You keep adding seconds, ephemeris and
    Standard Internationale and leap seconds,
To make reality fit your scheme.
    But the earth oscillates, the
    moon wobbles, the sun staggers
    across space where everything
    pulls and pushes and strains
    against the laws of gravity,
fighting to escape and be free.
    But your earth is locked tight
    between a star,
    a gray rock,
    and an air planet,
just as we are locked into
    our fuzzy memory of the past,
    our tenuous grasp of the present,
    and our feeble expectations of the future.

∞

Chapter 18

*I*ris's trouble was a hurricane that developed over the mid-Atlantic.

It turns out that the Romance languages are right. *Le temps/El tiempo/Il tempo* mean both time and weather. *Quel temps fait-il?* means 'What's the weather like?' In order to ask for the time you have to say *Quelle heure est-il?* But 'time flies' is *le temps vole*, which can also mean 'time steals.' I don't know how we manage to understand one another, in any language.

Iris kept speaking about parasites, parasites, even before she left the hospital. The doctors didn't know what to make of it. She had stopped nagging us about what time it was and about what day it was. I had left one of those calendars with a page for each date, writ large enough for her to see from across the room. I had also given her one of my watches, a French one with the Little Prince on its face that I had gotten years ago but didn't wear anymore. She loved it and wore it around her wrist, with the watch on the inside of her wrist.

If a patient thought she had parasites, she would surely gesture towards her guts, or perhaps rub her skin, maybe scratch her scalp. The linguist in me noticed that she used the French word, *parasite*, pronounced /pa/ra/zeet/, with the r trilled at the back of the throat.

She had said that her telesthesia was no longer working, in other words, her ability to know things from a distance and from a distance of time (funny, we have no such word! timelength? timefar? time-distance? timestance?) had lapsed. Her direct connection to Kronos had been garbled. Then I thought of her usage of parasite. She didn't mean a parasite of the body. The French make use of the same word to mean an electromagnetic perturbation, a noise, that superposes on a signal and makes it difficult or impossible to discern said signal, let alone understand it. English uses the word 'static' which, if you ask me, is just as illogical. Crackling that remains immobile? Electrical interference that doesn't move, even though the signal itself is moving at the speed of sound? No, that's not right. Radio waves are part of the group of electromagnetic radiation which includes light. Therefore, they all move very fast. But we cannot see radio waves with our eyes; we hear them with our ears. Had we different types of senses, this might be reversed. In any case, to return to the hissing and crepitation which degrade a radio signal, I believe the preferred term, static, is short for static electricity, but how it works—including linguistically—to create acoustic noise is beyond my ken. Still, radio frequencies disturbed by electromagnetic induction are a far cry from the interference that Iris was experiencing over the disruptions in her communications with Kronos.

Then it hit me: Was Kronos not only the god of time but also god of the weather? This gigantic storm that sat in the Atlantic like a white tarantula with its multiple legs curled in a counter-clockwise arrangement, every day creeping closer to Florida, was it the product of time, as in *tempus fugit*, but also the product of *temperature*, as in the increasing heat stored in the ocean? Was this a *tempest* whipped up to a sizzling *tempo* as physics played out its danse macabre, fulfilling its foul *temperament*, heat rising, twisted into a foul *temper* by the motion of the planet around its axis, the heated atmosphere retaining more and more moisture, electrons flowing and accumulating and seeking to discharge their, well, charge? It was inevitable.

So, it seems, was its projected route. The computer models all forecast the storm to graze the eastern part of Cuba, then travel up the Florida peninsula. Not known was the initial point of impact: Key Largo? South Beach? Palm Beach?

Judging by Iris's mounting sense of apprehension, I was sure the hurricane would make landfall right over our heads.

We had a couple of days to prepare. The hospital discharged Iris as soon as it could do so legally. The staff needed to hunker down with the sickest of the patients and they needed to make room for all those pregnant ladies past twenty weeks who needed to ride out the storm at the hospital. It wasn't that the low barometric pressure of the hurricane was thought to induce labor, but rather to avoid having those who went prematurely into labor attempt to brave the storm to get to the hospital.

George decided that he preferred to ride out the storm with friends who lived inland. He took de Naïf with him. I was left holding Iris's hand.

"Iris," I told her. "You're going to have to come home with me. You don't have a choice. I live in unincorporated Miami-Dade County, in a tiny neighborhood bordered by three giants, Coconut Grove to the east, Coral Gables to the north and southeast, and South Miami to the west and southwest. The good thing is that my property is smack on the Coastal Atlantic Ridge, seventeen feet above sea level. We'll be safe there, I assure you. No storm surge will hit us that far inland. I've ridden out many storms there. My house is safe."

Iris's neck muscles moved as if they were spasming. She clasped and unclasped her hands. But she said not a word as she was wheeled out of her room.

I had a nurse wait next to her wheelchair by the front door of the hospital while I went to get my car. In a few minutes, Iris was standing by my car, but unwilling to get into the passenger seat.

"Please, Iris," I said to her. "You must come with me. I cannot leave you on the Beach. It will not be safe for you here." I tried in all the languages we shared.

She stood as if glued to the sidewalk. It was evident that this was a momentous decision for her. She hadn't left the Beach in years. She went west only as far as Belle Isle, and north only as far as Lincoln Road Mall. What I was asking her to do was completely out of her comfort range.

I had an idea.

"Is Kronos communicating with you now?"

I knew what the answer would be.

"No," she replied, her face dark and agitated as if Kronos had forsaken her forever and she didn't know why.

"Then come with me," I said. "Maybe Kronos won't realize that you've come away from South Beach. What with the storm and all…"

I assumed that the hurricane was the culprit in the disruption of their communication. "Come with me. I promise that as soon as the storm passes, I'll bring you back to the Beach, as soon as the roads are passable. If not, I'll rent a boat in the Grove and we'll cross the bay to get to the Beach."

This seemed to calm her agitated nerves. She looked right into my eyes, trying to surmise my sincerity. I meant what I had said, so I had nothing to worry about. She relented.

I helped her into the passenger seat, passing the seatbelt in front of her and bending over her to attach it on her left side. As I did so, she kissed me on the cheek. I felt like a hero, helping the damsel in distress. I smiled at her.

"Don't worry, *belle dame*. We'll be fine. You'll see. We'll be fine. I live in a strong house. It's seen many storms. Many storms."

She didn't seem nervous as we crossed Biscayne Bay on the MacArthur Causeway. I felt as strong as the guy the causeway was named for, General Douglas MacArthur, as I carried Iris away from peril. It wasn't until we reached the Miami side that a bit of my resolve began to waver. Dear Lord. I certainly hoped that everything would be okay. The eye of the storm was only two days away and we were already feeling the outer bands, with long periods of heavy rain interspersed with squalls. Edouard, they were calling him. Even if he veered to the west or to the east, we were still going to get a major part of his strong gusts. But if Edouard veered to the west, we would get the worst of his winds.

With Edouard uppermost in my mind, I forgot all about Kronos.

Chapter 19

*I*t was interesting to introduce Iris to Lucy, my cat.

We were standing in the kitchen, trying to decide if I should go to the stores for last-minute items. I certainly needed to go buy Iris some clothes. All she brought with her was what she had had at the hospital. But I was doubting that I had the courage to go shopping two days before the storm hit. The stores would be teeming with agitated, brusque people, not to say irrational people, who grapple with others to get things they don't even need. The apocalyptic mind loses all sense of decorum, sympathy or solicitude for others, and, well, sense itself. An overwrought instinct for survival focuses their strategy, but not their reasoning. Some on the coast will drown from the storm surge, but they'll have in their pantries twenty bottles of ketchup, thirty bags of Doritos, and an untold number of soggy rolls of toilet paper.

Lucy came into the kitchen and sprang up on one of the bar chairs. As usual, her eyes darted around uncontrollably, as if she had nystagmus, not looking directly at us but in our general vicinity and focusing somewhere behind us. Iris immediately approached Lucy and began to caress her. She spoke to her in a language I had never heard her speak before and which I could not identify. Lucy closed her eyes and purred.

I decided not to leave the house and brave the crowds at the stores. The last time I had done that, several hurricanes ago, I found frenzy and chaos and empty shelves. The only water available was Evian. I'm a francophile, so I bought it. I might lose power and be in the dark for a couple of weeks, but at least I would be assuaging my thirst in style. After that experience, I always maintain a rational hurricane supply center in my pantry: battery-operated radio, extra batteries for it and the flashlights, bottled water, canned goods, manual can opener, candles, chocolate and a first aid kit. I have a gas range, so even if we lost power we'd be able to eat hot food. I also have a generator, with enough gas to last a couple of weeks.

Iris was content to stay in the living room watching the approach of Edouard through the French doors. In the meantime, I did a couple of loads of laundry and one of the dishwasher. The following day, the day before the hurricane was expected to make landfall, I closed the shutters, lashed the library doors together upstairs, threw the outside furniture into the pool, and brought the potted plants into the pool house. I knew I would be amused chasing after lizards and tree frogs for days afterwards, but at least I knew the plants wouldn't be blown away.

Then the moment arrived when both Iris and I sat hypnotized by the meteorological reports on TV, changing channels to hear the freshest bulletins about the hurricane. Edouard was huge. He had clipped the eastern part of Cuba, causing havoc and deaths, at least fifteen, at last count. Its eye was still south-east of the Bahamas and already we had perpetually dark skies and forceful gusts. The Beach, of course, always has a mandatory evacuation, and the views of the traffic leading out on all the causeways were eerie and spectacular. I wondered if Iris thought that we had gotten away in the nick of time.

She was strangely quiet as the skies lit up with lightning and the winds began to dishevel the tallest plants, the oaks, the palms and the bananas. As night approached, the powerful winds became sustained, with no relief at any time. Then came the sounds I hate the most, the sounds transmitted through the interior walls of the house itself: the shudder of the outside walls, violent thuds from the roof, scratching and scraping of tree branches from everywhere as the pressure of the gusts built up, it all echoed down to us on the first floor. The wind whistled, howled, moaned, and the compression of the air lay heavily on us, forcing us down on our chairs. Around three in the morning, the power went off. The generator came on immediately, but we lost the TV anyway since the whole system would have needed to be rebooted. I decided that it was best if we didn't know what Edouard was doing. Its eye was still south of us, which meant that we hadn't gotten the brunt of its brutal strength. If only we could fall asleep and magically awaken after it had passed over us.

But who could go to sleep with all that racket? Things were breaking in the garden. We heard glass shattering, but it couldn't be from my house since it has impact resistant windows. It was probably stuff landing on us from the houses around. Every half hour I would walk the whole house, looking for damage to the windows. There was none. But water was coming in under the doors facing east. I packed towels at their base to keep the seepage in check.

The wind made the outside walls vibrate. They shook with fury, as if we were having an earthquake. Novels always say that the wind howls, including mine just a couple of paragraphs ago. This wind was screeching, at high pitch, like ten thousand witches yelling in unison. The witches were also hitting the house with their brooms, all ten thousand of them at the same time. Thuds, bangs, rumbles, knocks, booms, all matter of noises resounded from all directions, especially the roof. We could feel changes in pressure, too. All the windows were tightly closed yet we could still feel a hot humid breeze inside the house, coming across the first-floor hallway and ending in the kitchen where Iris and I were holed up. Even though there are huge windows in the kitchen, they face west so I didn't think we were in any danger. Besides, I had great confidence in my impact-resistant windows.

Iris was strangely calm. She sat by the kitchen island, taking sips of her Earl Grey tea, her eyes made bright by the flashes of lightning which also showed momentary snippets of the trees outside in dramatic positions, especially the palm trees which were doubled over. Every lightning bolt delineated a world in violent motion, as if wrecking balls were swinging down from the sky.

But there was another sound, a rather peaceful one, that could be heard from all directions around the house: the ubiquitous tree frogs sustained their rhythmic croaking throughout the night. Didn't they have enough sense to be terrorized? Could they really be content to be amidst those hellish suroundings? It wasn't until nearly dawn that they decided to shut up. By that time, the winds began to die down as well. Iris and I went into the media room and fell on the couches. I fell immediately into a deep sleep.

Chapter 20

When I woke up, Iris was not on her couch. I found her outside in the garden.

Or what was left of it. At first I was relieved to see Iris, but the sight of my demolished garden sent twinges of pain into my soul. My sapodilla was down, the bamboo were down, the bananas weren't down, but they weren't where they were supposed to be, either. They were just gone. The key lime had also disappeared.

The bushes growing next to the walls were all toppled over, the wind having traveled down the sides of the house to knock them down perpendicularly away from the walls. But the windows had held, including those of the pool house. The pool itself was murky with hundreds of branches. Ah, I found the key lime!

Iris was standing close to the border of the garden behind the pool, looking towards the west. As I approached her, I saw that she was smiling.

"He's speaking to me again," she announced.

I understood it to be Kronos. "So, it's okay that you're away from the Beach?"

"Yes, it is. He understands. We would have been in danger had we stayed on the Beach. You were right. They had an 18-foot storm surge."

"We would have definitely been in trouble had we stayed. I hope he understands that we won't be able to go back immediately. Even if we decide to go back by boat, the roads in the Grove will be closed. The streets will be impassable on the Beach. They might still be underwater. You don't mind if we wait a day or two before making the attempt to go back?"

She shook her head. "That's fine. I have things to write."

I understood. Now that the Kronos connection was back, things were again being dictated to her.

We went back inside. The garden could wait. The important thing was to make sure that Iris had plenty of writing paper and her choice of writing tools. She wrote for hours. Every time I would bring her something to drink or to eat, I stole a glance or two at the papers arrayed on the dining room table. I could identify different languages. I even identified a few sheets written in the Cyrillic alphabet. Inwardly I groaned. How was I going to have those translated? Moreover, was I even going to be privy to them? I had no idea who the recipients were.

When Iris went to the bathroom, I took advantage and took pictures of as many pages as I dared to.

I need not have worried. Afterwards I found out that she had written the same poetry in seven languages: English, French, Creole, Spanish, Portuguese, German and Russian. For what purpose, I never knew. Were they intended for individuals? When and where was she going to hand them out? I'm glad I took the photos, for I never saw those sheets of paper again.

One of the poems written after the hurricane, the English version:

∞

> What kind of animal fouls its own nest?
> A brute with no instinct of self-preservation,
> Using, taking, using up, taking over,
> Possessive, heedless, destructive, indifferent,
> Sapiens as a name is irony and shame:
> Where is the wisdom in what this species does?
> No frontal-lobe planning,
> No cerebral consideration,

No intuitive concerns over
The destruction of his mother
That leads to his own.

Now the earth moves on,
Her geologic time moves her spine
In a great frisson:
Mountains quake, seas move in,
Ocean currents stop, back up,
Invert their salinity equations as
Continents freeze, glaciers slide,
Deserts enlarge, encroach and hide
The sabotage of man,
Homo sapiens idioticus.

Chapter 21

*I*t took a couple of hours, but we finally got back to South Beach, days later.

In ordinary times, it takes forty minutes to get from my house to South Beach, but with so many lanes blocked, it was slow going.

George and de Naïf reappeared. Iris went to live with them again. The streets of the Beach were terribly unsafe, what with debris and stinking dead fish and pools of water on which floated films of beautifully irridescent blue, gold, green and gray swirls. I saw a handgun in a gutter. On West Avenue and Fifth there was a broken baby grand piano festooned with tree branches. It must have been sucked out of a high-rise condo. What happened to the piano player? Tree limbs were the most prevalent of detritus, still scattered all around, but most of them had been pulled to form little hills on the edges of streets, allowing cars to meander between them as best they could.

No power, yet. Climbing up to George's tenth-floor flat made us fight for breath, especially those of us with grocery bags in our arms. The hot and steamy weather that usually follows a hurricane put us all out of sorts. As soon as we were all inside we opened the windows wide open to let in a slight breeze.

There was debris even on George's balcony. De Naïf amused himself by kicking it through the railings and watching it fall all the way down to the ground. Iris joined him at the balcony, looking out over the leafless terrain of South Beach. There was no green any more. What leaves were visible were plastered on all the walls and windows of neighboring buildings. Iris looked to the horizon with a grim expression, although I could also detect a certain satisfaction in her eyes and in the way her mouth was set. It was the look of, "Yeah, I told you, things are going badly and they're going to get worse, just like I predicted. It's only a matter of time."

We made sandwiches and emptied George's refrigerator. What was still edible, we ate; the rest went into the garbage. We had no idea when the garbage pickup would be reinstated. This part of the process, we already knew from experience, was just as bad as the storm. Things were going to get a lot smellier and stickier before they got better.

I do remember a hurricane, though, that passed through South Florida years ago and the very next day a cold front swept through. That was weird, to have cool weather right after a hurricane. Most of the time, post-hurricane was a time for sweltering, sweating and swearing in irritable depression and surly lethargy.

Knowing this, as soon as I saw that Iris was as comfortable as she could be, I flew the coop. I had a generator back home to return to. I also needed to continue editing Iris's book. It was coming together more or less logically. Some of the material could fit into two or more categories, so the final placement of certain poems at times gave the impression of arbitrary arrangement, even—I'll admit it—becoming a bit chaotic in several places. I was convinced, however, that the themes themselves were chaotic, describing confusion, terror, entropy. Apocalyptic occurrences have a tendency to do that. Terra firma becoming aquatic, the water destroying your entire house, all your belongings, drowning your loved ones with you unable to save them, knowing that you're next, leads to a state of mind necessarily bewildered. One day you are worried about a certain meeting you have to go to on the following morning, then the next day you can't go to work at all because your car is in the flooded garage. But if you survive, the worry about the meeting lingers, until the water enters your home, then you have bigger things to worry about. Still, you wonder if your house, your neighborhood, the entire city, will ever get back to normal. This wasn't the story of the Titanic, deemed to be unsinkable, but it still became a tomb for hundreds of people; this was you at home, in a place of safety and comfort, and the water came to kill you there. Similarly to the victims of the Titanic, you also believed in the impossibility of such a catastrophe visiting your home. But it turns out that neither the Titanic nor the Florida barrier islands and low coasts were unsinkable. Tough destiny to accept, especially when your finances, your life, your past, your purloined future are all so inextricably conjoined to the land. Then the land disappears. Water replaces it. Your regular life ebbs away.

For us at this moment, however, things slowly returned to normal. Streets dried up, were cleared of detritus, trees sprouted new leaves, even those that were still partially uprooted and lying on their backs. Homeowners contacted insurers who contacted contractors and soon business was abuzz with hammering and power sawing and painting, with everyone enthusiastically concentrating on the repairs and the return to normal. Humans are the best at self-delusions and irrational fantasies. They rebuild on the very spot where, eventually, they will be taken down.

Chapter 22

*I*ris redoubled her efforts to make others believe that normal was valid no more.

Her poems became more visceral, her message more dire. Death and destruction ran down the pen along with the ink and sprayed the pages with pathetic portaits of submerged people, overwhelmed by a series of low tidal waves that kept increasing in height until the first floor of every building was engulfed. For those living in houses with only one floor, if they didn't outsmart the waves to clamber onto their roofs, they drowned while pounding on their ceilings. In the lowest of areas, the second story was inundated as well. In multi-story buildings, the first-floor dwellers had to ask people higher up if they could be taken into their apartments. In some buildings, those living in the highest floors looked down so much on the people living closer to the ground that they refused to take them in. These weren't regular floods, they said. These floods were not going to dissipate in a few days, even a few weeks. These floods were here to stay. They didn't have enough food or water for other people. This was the new normal.

Some of Iris's poems described the future of the residents on the higher floors. Perhaps they weren't the more fortunate ones. They would survive the initial inundations, but after months of no electricity, tired of clambering up and down staircases, they would succumb to all sorts of human ails. Any sort of wound festered without antibiotics. Without their regular medication, many were doomed. The stress of living in a perpetual flood brought on heart attacks. Mostly they died of hunger. When their hurricane pantry provisions ran out, there was no way to replenish them. They gave up soon thereafter. The unlucky ones had pets, which they ate, even though it only gave them sustenance for a few more days. The water from the taps had run for a few weeks, then the water turned murky. Some people continued drinking it and died of intestinal ailments. People rigged plastic shower curtains to catch rainwater from their terraces, but that was only temporary as well. Some managed to catch fish or snare birds on their terrace. Many did not care to continue living life like this and took their own lives. Life, apparently, at least for the most spoiled and least tenacious among us, is worth living only when electricity runs from outlets and water from spigots.

Funny, I'm telling this part of the story in the past, as if it already happened. But these events were all still very much into the future. Iris continued writing poems to people about their future.

I asked Iris why she hadn't written a poem for me, to tell me about my own future, about my own death.

She fixed her blue eyes directly into mine and answered, "You're too close to me. I see you every day, almost, and I speak to you every day, on the phone, on the days I don't see you. There are many emotions within you that I elicit; you feel too much for me. You worry, you fret, you look for me on the streets with concern, you look after me when you can. It is written all over your face. Your anxiety about me creates a halo of disturbance as strong as bad weather. Kronos cannot tell me anything about you, just as he cannot tell me about my own future. We're either too close to him, or we give off too much interference. We static each other." This was my translation of her weird sentence in French: Nous nous parasitons.

"For instance," she continued, "before, when de Naïf used to accompany me on my deliveries, I couldn't tell his future. But now that he has been spending all his time with George, his future is beginning to emerge more clearly. It is becoming less obstructed, and I can see him leaving with George. They will leave the island in the nick of time. George is even going to be able to sell his flat. They believe what I have been writing, and their fear will propel them to leave. With you, before, I could see you staying in your big house on the Ridge. But now I cannot see that. Yet I doubt that you would come to the island, even for my sake. Your house is big and safe and you belong there. So long as you protect it from marauders, you should be safe."

"And you," I asked her. "You have never been able to see any detail about your own future?"

"None at all. Kronos will not, but maybe he cannot, see into my future because I am too close to him. I am his oracle and because of that I think I will be kept safe."

"Well, whatever happened to the Oracle at Delphi?"

"The Sibyls were attacked, first by the Persians, then by the Gauls. Both times, the seers were killed or enslaved. This means that Kronos did not warn them of the danger ahead of time. It must seem that a clairvoyant is a fraud if she cannot see her own future, her own demise, but it is Kronos who allows her to see her future or who hides it from her."

"I suppose being a clairvoyant is a thankless job. You help other people, but in the end, who helps the clairvoyant?"

"Not even another clairvoyant."

"You mean, there are more of you?"

"There are. There are many of us, in many lands. We all try to do the same thing, but too many people disbelieve us. That is the way it has always been. Cassandra was one of us, and her society wrote about her. But nobody writes about us now."

"Well, I will. I will write about you."

"I thought you were just collecting my glances into the future."

"That is what I was planning, but you just convinced me that

I need to write about you, too. Maybe more people will believe what you predict if they get to know you better."

"Cassandra's society knew very well about her. They knew about her prophecies, they knew that they had all come to pass. And yet they neglected her at the most crucial moment. They allowed the wooden horse to be brought in. And hidden within it was their own death."

I agreed with her. "It was their own hubris. They thought that they had defeated the enemy and became intoxicated by their victory. It could not dawn on them that they had not been victorious. A woman, however wise and knowledgeable were she, could not in the remotest stretches of the imagination uncloud their vision. In their paroxysms of self-delusion and egotistical fantasies, they would never have been led to the belief that they were soon to experience defeat, and death. To believe that the enemy had left them a parting gift before they ran away with their tails between their legs must be the epitome of self-delusion. They probably thought that the enemy had been generous out of respect and admiration!"

"Well," answered Iris, "what you see these days may be worse. Man has deluded himself into believing the planet he has always abused will forever continue to be benevolent and generous towards him. But you see, everything has an end. Gaia has shuddered in reaction to the torment man has unleashed on her. She will rearrange her hair and change her pose. This will alter oceans, move mountains, create new configurations of continents. The world's biota will change once again. Most species will die, but the race will be on in a different category and in a different direction, with man a sorry absence. One has to accept the conclusion that he deserves his fate. Man has known for a long time that he has been destroying his planet. But his days as a parasite are coming to an end."

"I know what you mean, Iris. I know what you mean. And I agree with you."

After a pause I said, "Man is selfish and can't see that the harm he's done to the earth will now come back to destroy him. Yet, he refuses to accept his complicity in his own demise. Blind he is, stuck-up blind."

Iris looked at me with deep sadness. "He will die blind. Here, as in all coasts, the water will come to drown him. In other places, the tiniest of life forms will infect him and kill him. In still other places, the rains will stop and dry up his food supply and he will starve to death. Nature is about to make a concerted effort to rid herself of this most dangerous parasite. Man accepts only the idea that he was placed on earth in order to receive Her bounty. He likes to view himself as Master of his domain. He doesn't like to think of himself as a parasite. But all the evidence points to the fact that he is a parasite, the worst there has ever been, for he destroys his world."

"Kronos doesn't believe there is any hope for—?" I began to ask Iris.

She interrupted me. "No hope. It's too late." She snickered. "Way too late. The time has come for men to go."

Poem on death and destruction:

∞

The Weight of Water

Neptune's child is not the Kraken
for it is rather a local monster.
No, the monster who sleeps
Awakens drop by drop, each a tentacle

reaching towards the sea to add
    its weight in flows and currents.
It is the ice, frozen in place for eons,
    which stirs, in rivulets and eddies,
Adding drop by drop, drip by drip,
    to the volume of the sea.
The Whiteness is gone, which reflected to space
    the sun's rays that now penetrate deep
into the soil and the warmth seeps down,
    the tundra is unlocked
and releases the water down
    the land and into the sea
      the swollen   sea
the rising   sea, heavy   with
    movement   liquid gravity
dancing   with winds   bracing
    with breezes   ocean cliffs
     flowing down
southern   latitudes and
    throwing their weight   onto   the coasts
     tentacles moving   in wild
directions   covering   covering
    a liquid   lid, heavy   and thick.
The Kraken   has been   released
    everywhere at once.

∞

Chapter 23

*I*ris was delivering a hundred portents a day.

She wrote all morning long, getting up at dawn, ending around noon. She was still at George's flat, having considered the time she saved by not having to scramble for meals, thankful for the constant flow of writing implements. She also saved time in the evenings, especially on rainy nights, when she didn't have to seek dry accommodations in a threshold or under a bridge.

Her clients, or her "souls," as she called them, had changed in their aspect. Tourists had more or less abandoned the Beach as hotels brought their facilities up to snuff and the city normalized its transportation schedules. Instead, a different type of person had flooded into the area: disaster-relief workers. First responders from as far away as Vermont, California, Canada, Argentina, Mexico and Belgium rushed in, coming in by rescue boats, trucks, buses and planes, bringing in medical supplies and generators, bottled water, food, temporary shelters that popped up in Flamingo Park, electrical and plumbing equipment, amphibious vehicles and portable surgical units. There were medical personnel, FEMA workers, emergency-response managers, epidemiologists, tree-removal experts, construction people, charity representatives, health and safety inspectors, building inspectors, in short, a plethora of new blood for Iris. She had never been busier.

I still couldn't drive in. Besides the remaining debris, there was still way too much activity on the streets of Miami Beach. The parking lots had become temporary deposit areas for the detritus. They filled the air with the pungent odor of vegetation fermenting under the blazing sun. I had to take water taxis from the Grove and walk the rest of the way, so I wasn't seeing too much of Iris. Also, even though the power had come back, George's individual a/c unit wasn't working. What's more, the editing process that I was working on with Clara was proceeding at a vertiginous pace. We had more than enough material and I didn't even want to see the new stuff that Iris was distributing. Perhaps later, for a second book. Would there be time for a second book, that is. Was there time for the first book?

Chapter 24

Our semester was just gearing up for midterms when George flew the coop.

I couldn't believe that he wasn't even waiting for the end of the semester. How could he abandon his students? I had never heard of a teacher leaving his classes in the middle of the semester.

"It's about to start," he told me over the phone. "Great timing, too," he added. "Just closed on the sale of the condo this morning, so I would need to vacate it promptly anyway."

"Somebody just bought your place?" I asked him, not quite understanding what he was telling me.

"Yeah, can you believe it? What unbelievable luck!"

I thought to myself: he calls it luck when somebody has just bought a place in a building that is soon to be flooded up to the third floor.

"Where are you moving to?" I asked him.

"North Carolina. Blue Ridge Mountains. We'll be safe there." Then he changed his mind and added, *"Safer.* We'll be safer there than here, that's for sure. Iris was a bit fuzzy about North Carolina, but she said that the problem up there will be with all the people streaming in from the coast."

"You said it's about to start?"

"Yes. Iris spent the night at my place and she was moaning and groaning about the end being nigh, the waters are coming, what are they going to do, where are they going to go. She was fidgety as hell. She couldn't stop moving, pacing, rocking, swaying. We left her in the living room and went to sleep."

"De Naïf is with you?"

"Yes, of course. He's coming with me to North Carolina."

"And Iris?"

"I don't know about Iris. I hate leaving her, but she refuses to come with us. Told us she can't leave the Beach, that she has to stay here till the bitter end. I tried, and believe me, so did de Naïf, in all the languages they know together. He was even crying. We tried to convince her to come with us. But she wouldn't budge."

"But she's sure that it's about to start?"

"She's acting as if she was sure."

"Is she still there?"

"Nah. She left right after breakfast. De Naïf and I are packing the car. We're taking only what fits. The rest, I'm leaving behind. I was supposed to leave the condo empty, but what are they going to do, sue me? They're going to have bigger problems sooner than they think. By the way, I found out that Iris gave the buyers their predictions. Apparently, their fate was strong because they were somehow connected to me. They did read her pieces of paper, and thanked her. But then they did what most people have done: they put their prognostications in their pockets, there to stay, I'm afraid. So I don't feel that bad. She did try to warn them. But they bought the condo anyway. What people do with important information is their prerogative."

The fate of the new owners of George's flat was appalling, but I was more worried about Iris.

"Where is she now?"

"I don't know. She walked away without saying a word. Didn't take any pieces of paper with her, either. She just left, with nothing in her hands. I don't think she means to warn people anymore."

"Well, no. Not if the time has come." As an afterthought, I added, "It's too late for warnings."

"She said it'll start a bit after midnight, tonight. She said we'd have plenty of time to leave the city, if we left before noon. Not that there'll be a mad exodus of people bolting for I-95 and the Turnpike. However, she said we need to leave by noon because all of the Turnpike and most of I-95 will be flooded soon after midnight, so I want to be in Georgia asap. I think I'll take the Turnpike. Yup, I better."

I said nothing.

"So…" George hesitated. "I guess… this is it. I'll still have my cell phone, but I don't know for how long cell phones will work. In any case, you take care. Be safe."

"You, too, George," I answered. "Drive safely. Don't drive too fast."

"I won't. But Iris saw us living in North Carolina, so I don't have to worry."

"Still, the future isn't all that certain, so be careful."

"I will. You, too. Bye."

And he hung up the phone.

Chapter 25

$\mathcal{I}$ finished my afternoon classes and then went looking for Iris.

I drove in ready to spar with tractors and hauling vehicles, but it wasn't that bad. I even managed to find parking by the water, by South Pointe Beach.

I didn't do this on purpose. I had no idea where I would be able to find Iris. I just wanted to leave the car as close to the MacArthur Causeway as possible, for a quick exit, if need be. But as soon as I walked to the base of the South Pointe Park Pier, I saw her.

It was close to sunset and she was on the beach. Not hard to find at all: her long blond hair caught the warm yellow light of the setting sun.

She was staring off into that mesmerizing line between earth and sea. Only a few container ships broke the line of demarcation, now fading fast with the waning of the light.

There were other people out walking, enjoying the cooler air, the fading rays that gathered around the setting sun into a roiling Gordian knot of colors, from purple to peach to red, orange and yellow. Every day a beautiful sunset on Miami Beach, quite a tourist attraction, all due to a combination of the swirl of Saharan dust carried over the Atlantic and the particles of exhaust fume that waft up from heavy traffic in the city.

Of course, she wasn't surprised to see me. She began speaking to me of a subject in *medias res:* it was what she was thinking about at the moment.

"Man is so silly to think solely of time in a certain way: how time affects him only in the recent past, in the present, and the near future. Oh, some might think of preparing for their retirement, still

fifty years away, but very few. Some get stuck on an event that
happened fifty years ago, but again, very few. most focus on the
dwindling time between yesterday, today and tomorrow. Three
days. Three days that affect them, that interest them, so they say.
The rest of time, they ignore. You know, very few professions study
time. There's archaeology, of course, and geology, astronomy, and
anthropology, especially physical anthropology, and linguistic
anthropology. How far does the word 'rose' go and under what
versions, and do the obsolete, forgotten names smell as sweet?"

I responded, "An iris by any other name would look as lovely."

She smiled. "You only have to look around you to see the
evidence of the epochs. These far-reaching ages that span millions,
if not billions of years. Man has no imagination, and no desire to
find out. He is content to live life in the yesterday/today/tomorrow
sequence. If he takes quick glances into the past it's mostly out of
fear: too much nostalgia brings the understanding that you're that
much closer to your end. And if he looks ahead, it is mostly to
anticipate this summer's vacation, the start of the school year in
the fall. Look around, man, look around! The heavens show with
the speed of light the changes that abound in all the galaxies. But
that's too far out for people to fathom. Closer in, on terrestrial time,
there are rock strata to look into: evidence of turmoil and
catastrophe point to the possibility of the same in our time.
Dendrochronology does the same, in closer time. Tree rings mark
the good decades, and the bad ones. But there is something else,
something else that can be studied, that yields so much information
from a past that touches on man directly."

She waited for me to ask what it was, but when I remained
silent, she continued.

"It's evolutionary DNA. The study of the evolution of the
genetic code will unwrap the secrets of life, like a slow remembering

of the unreeling versions of man, sort of like peeling back the layers of an onion. In all life forms, the double helix of DNA incontrovertibly shows the previous life forms that make up its components. It's like a permanent palimpsest of the being's composite avatars, standing in line, transforming from one to the other, revealing what the being once was, and what it now is, all the way to the present. There is no hiding from your ancestors. They're all there, firmly standing in line—such a patient family!—for millions of years, and the fetus pays attention to them, for it goes through all the permutations, obeying the DNA's orders to pass through the fish stage, then the amphibian, the reptilian, the mammalian, and, if the creature is us, the humanoid stages, one by one, in breathtaking sequence. At moments, we have a tail, then we grow gills, then lose them, then we are covered in fur. It's called lanugo. Some preemies are born with it. Our nine months in the womb are a recapitulation of our genetic components, a time line of sorts, vast, almost imponderable. Many won't ponder it. They refuse it. They refuse both the time, because they have official documentation, their Bible, that shows them that we are much younger, and they refuse to accept that we are but an agglomeration of avatars. We have lived on this earth, through this device, in these volatile environments, countless times before. But man finds it hard to view such vast sweeps of time, and such complexity, in his own genesis. Man is afraid of infinity, yet he everywhere faces it. He prefers to believe in comforting mythologies.

"Man has an expiration date, so does our Earth, so, too, the Sun and the Galaxy in which it travels. But the Universe, or rather, the Universes, go on forever, in all dimensions, height, breadth, width, but also in the dimension of time. Sometimes time goes on by itself, without the accompaniment of spatial dimensions. Just time, pure, clean, detached, without requiring any space at all.

"If you're in a room full of blazing light, the photons don't push you to the walls. No, you're free to roam in a room full of light, and the light is everywhere at once, some of its wavelengths even going through you. That is in essence what time is. It is everywhere but doesn't need any space for it to be. If you could only open your eyes to see, you will find it everywhere around you. It is even inside you, in every cell of your being, in every neuron of your brain, in every mitochondria, in every red blood cell. Expand your vision to see it, and understand the wondrous power of it. Everything else is subordinated to it, controlled by it, determined by it. That whole civilizations fall underneath its carriage wheels is immaterial. Whole species succumb to it, to say nothing of the gods.

"Ah, what human illusions! Zeus becomes Deus; Amun, Jupiter, Jehova, Jesus, Allah, Quetzalcóatl, and so on and so forth; they all light up the sky like fireflies, and as ephemerally."

Iris looked up at the stars as if straining to see these blinking little lights, to no avail.

I, too, looked up, hoping to see our lightning bugs, but this beautiful insect, called the Devil's bug by some because of its two conspicuous "eyes" on its "forehead" that glow with eerie phosphorescence, scares some people. I remember as a kid they were everywhere in Miami. These days, if I see one a year, it's a cause for celebration. But I'm sure those who were spooked by this strange flying insect do not mourn its passing.

Yet gods were everywhere in the gloaming, invisible of course, flitting here and there, vying for importance, struggling for endurance, striving for remembrance, but one by one the dark lights flitted out like Devil's bugs succumbing to pesticides. Nothing was left but the dark clouds that now covered the whole dome of the sky, east to west, north to south. A breeze had sprung up and I felt chilled.

"Come with me, Iris. Please come with me. Stay with me. You liked my place. During the hurricane you said you liked it."

"I do like your place, and I like you immensely. You'll go back home and there you'll be safe. I have foreseen this. Go home. You'll be safe, I promise."

"I believe you, Iris, I do. But that means that you won't be safe if you stay here. Remember what you've said, the Beach, the whole eastern coast up to Nova Scotia will be inundated. Why don't you come with me, and you'll be safe, too. We'll be safe together."

"I can't, I can't leave with you. I can't leave this place. I feel..."

"Yes?" I looked pleadingly at her. "You feel..."

"I feel that this is the destiny I must follow."

"Like the captain of a sinking ship? Iris, You're not responsible for this place, for any of this, for the coming flood... You can't be blamed for what is about to happen."

Iris laughed. "I'm not like a captain. But I do know that people always blame the messenger. I'm sorry you weren't able to publish your book before the calamity came upon us. Perhaps more people would have paid attention. But you go ahead. Go home, where you'll be safe. I will feel better, knowing that you're safe."

She looked out over the ocean from which the first waves were to begin creeping up. It was completely dark already, but the lights of the city cast a lurid gleam on the water close to the beach. Farther off, towards the dark horizon between cloudy sky and murky sea, the night looked menacing, but only because of what we were anticipating.

"At what time is it supposed to begin?" I asked.

"The first few waves, cresting at only a few inches, will start around twoish. But the troughs will get deeper, and the wavelengths shorter, around 3:30. By 4, the waves that begin to enter people's homes will start their destruction. By 5, most of the people who are supposed to drown will be drowned. Sunrise will show the survivors the stunning sight of their city underwater. It's mostly the high-rise people who will see this, and it will not dawn on them immediately that they are the unlucky ones. Poor people. I tried to warn them. I tried so hard."

"Some people did heed. They took precautions. They took steps."

"Very few, very few. Most people have to see with their own eyes, with their very own eyes. But by then, it's way too late. The thing is over."

"Yet you showed them the signs. They should have seen the signs."

"Modern people don't look for the signs any more. They confuse ancient reliance on omens and portents, eclipses and shooting stars, with scientifically-based observations of changing natural events. The coincidence of a shooting star cannot be compared with the shaving-brush tree flowering earlier and earlier every year for decades. The star comes and goes fortuitously. The tree represents a trend, but the trend is not motivating enough for most people. They have their lives, their real estate, their kids at a good school. Moving is such a nuisance. Human self-delusion has no bounds."

"Iris, please. Come with me."

At that very moment, I felt water lapping at my shoe. I looked down and so did Iris.

"Ah, here it is, the very first baby wave that's going to eventually kill millions and change the coasts forever."

We had only been standing a couple of feet from the lapping waves. But this miniature wave did not recede. Instead, about thirty seconds later, a second wave came up from the dark sea and sent water over my shoes. I stepped back.

"There, you see?" laughed Iris with child-like glee. "It has started. A bit early."

She also walked onto dry sand. I was about to open my mouth but she cut me short.

"No, no, you go, you go. Thank you for your protection these past few months. I appreciate it so much."

Tears sprang up from my eyes as I realized that Iris was going to stay. I stepped closer to her and gathered her into my arms. It was a big embrace, long enough to be uncomfortable for her, I knew, but this was going to be the last time I ever saw Iris. A thought flitted through my mind that I could just take her in my arms and run to the parking lot. But no. I had to respect the sanctity of her decision, the resolution of her will. I had to leave Iris there on this beach.

Another little wave lapped at our feet. It broke the concentration of my embrace.

"Good-bye, Iris," By this time, I felt my tears as copious as the waves.

"Good-bye, protector, defender of poetry, publisher of truth."

She said it with a smile. Then she added, "Take the MacArthur home. It'll be open for another couple of hours. You'll be safe at home. And do try to publish our book anyway. Perhaps it will help the people who remain. Maybe they'll see the errors of their ways, and start the change. For change they will have to do, if they want to keep the planet as their environment. Otherwise, they'll make a planet fit for other creatures who, perhaps, will in turn make the right decisions for themselves when their time comes to do so."

I nodded in agreement.

"I will publish your book, Iris. I'll find the way, even if I have to produce the whole thing myself."

I started walking away from her as another wavelet came foaming ashore, this time with a little more strength and speed. I walked onto dry sand, but she stayed in the water and gave me a little wave of her fingers. She turned around and waded a little more deeply into the charcoal-gray waters. I kept looking back as I walked to my car, seeing Iris step in the water deep enough to get the hem of her dress wet. After a while, it was only her blond hair that I could distinguish in the dark. Behind her, the horizon remained dark and infinite.

I was home in half an hour. There was hardly any traffic.

Epilogue

We in South Florida are hardly alone in the aftermath of the destruction.

Up and down the Atlantic coast, low-lying towns remain submerged in murky waters. Hundreds of thousands have died, but if you follow the coastline down into Central and South America, then the numbers rise into the millions. Strangely enough, the Pacific rim has not been affected as much, just archipelagoes like the Maldives and Vanuatu, which were in peril even before this new deluge. On our side of the world, Iceland has become a new archipelago. Venice is gone, as are most of the Netherlands.

In my neighborhood, the water is about a dozen blocks away. I can now smell the sea, when before I couldn't.

The Collected Poems of Iris Cornelia Starkaugen

∞

Mirages quiver through thick moist air,
Melt and tremble, splatter their matter on
Keen rods and cones frantic in their search, unwavering
On their rocky promontory so high
They think they reach closer to the light.

Wet air does not conduct images so well:
Photons, maybe bosons, rush to its edge and desist,
Cowards, from jumping into the abyss.
Metal does no better. Thicker, denser, hotter,
We scratch for it, purify it in fire, for electrons.

Yet time does the better job, it leaves our sight clear
Of twinkling and parasitic distortions.
In its circular elasticity it delivers visions
Unwavering, unsettling, direct to mind and heart.
Time is the best conductor of vision.

∞

Man is the pliant reed bending flat to the ground
As rain and hail pelt it, gales blast it, sun beats it;
Delicate botany, to have given the reed a flimsy stalk,
Weak vertebrae that bow down before adversity;
Whereas its roots are tenacious, digging deep
In their grip of a handful of moldering dirt.
Such resolve to cling to earth, even when life beats us
Down to oblivion.

∞

∞

The recipe for visions is clarity whisked with timelessness.
Time is a vulgar weed, but crush it and aerate it,
Make it rush by, make it stand still, do your bidding,
Then you see—stand still!—for this one second and for eons:
Mountains erode, so how can you hope to linger,
Sad sad chef.

∞

It is here, at the threshold between temperate zone
And solar flare tropics, on a barrier island,
That earth will see its primacy bend low to the rushing sea.
Here will the stage re-enact the blows that water throws on land,
Till the land, ragged and overrun, bloated under tropical suns,
Surrenders its dominance.

Such battles between land and sea are readily legible by geologists.
The vision to decipher the layers of eons past is written in stone.
In oolitic rock. Sedimentary limestone.
Look and read: read the stony Braille.
Once the story is felt and known,
It no longer even feels like war. It is but the play of titans.
The sea and the land gambol with each other.

The land grabs, falls back, then the sea swells, moves forward.
Drenched, the land runs amok,
Dried, the muck rakes back,
The sea falls, but with sun- and moontides behind it,
With the volume of the melted world's ice behind it,
The sea moves heavy with bulge and force.
The surge engulfs its playmate once again.

∞

∞

Row upon row of crosses and stars of David visible to the horizon.
Beyond is the onyx sea with a horizon of its own.
Horizon upon horizon of destinies and fates too numerous to disentangle.
We unwind, we unchain, we unravel.
Barbaric winds from the east, balmy breezes from the south,
We unwind, we unchain, we unravel.

Finistère. Land's End. Southernmost island. Westernmost point.
We stand at the edge, feeling entitled because we own this dirt.
You hold the deed high in your pyrrhic hand.
The land ignores us. It will elevate or sink, floating on thin crusts,
Itself the toy of forces too varied, too chaotic, to map out.
We are not even a nuance on the map, save for our scratching
And our stabbing, shoving and ramming and fracking.
It will be our turn next, when she shrugs.

Why do movies think the end will come tsunami-like, with starlets
And their paramours hugging beneath the crushing wave?
It will be more like the land being sucked under, tumbling fast
Beneath the surface of the sea. Then the sea will fill the void
From all directions, swallowing up the film sets as the cameras
Keep rolling.

∞

∞

I see the sands of time every day.
Enough sand to fill hourglasses for every man, woman and child.
I hold the sand in the palm of my hand.
There is enough energy here, as I let it pour through my fingers,
To wind clocks and watches till the ends of time.
There is more sand than time.
Each grain holds enough free space to shelter a universe.
Galaxies careen and supernovae explode within each speck,
Taking along in their gyrations small worlds filled with beings
Whose only succor is that they can think.

∞

Wingèd Kronos is my lover.
He is pliant, moves me to the past,
Hovers over the present until seconds
        become days;
He is achingly plangent as he sings to me
Of the future.
        I hear, I see, I know, I understand;
I am in the inside circle,
        the bearer of his news to those who are
Blind. They ignore the past, barely live
        the present, disregard the future,
forever lost to time.
Willfully blind they are to damages accrued,
Debts burgeoning, dues unsettled. It is
Unsettling. Kronos, my lover, generous
        and true, give them the sight to see.
Why only me?
Kronos my lover lets them view only the
        passage of time.
Soon there will be the settling of debts and the
        settling of souls. Kronos, what about
My soul?

∞

∞

I saw a tree being cut down today.
As busy men lent their attention low on the trunk,
The canopy shuddered, leaves fell, branches quaked.
When the tree's soul cracked, loud like a pistol shot, I gasped.
My eyes saw the trunk severed, the sap bleeding down to the ground,
As its foliage bent down with dignity and grace.
Then it was dismembered, shredded and chipped,
Hauled away. Its stump was ground down to below soil.
Nothing remained, save silence and an empty space.

∞

once upon a time waits for no one time stands
still stitch in time endless time after time and
again time is of the essence time be still time
flies lost time changes everything the time
has come in the fullness of time illusion of
time the great healer one more time there is a
time and place time will tell the time is ripe
in the nick of time is a river time on your
hands a matter of time wasted time is the
master love kills time time kills love spend
time no hand to catch time the first time the
last time take the time make up for lost time
heals time destroys time and tide killing time
no time like the present time and space the
time has passed past time lost time
regained time recalled a race against time.
time's up.

∞

We bear witness to the passage of time/we rage/
we decry/we show our scars/fists raised in outrage/
the game is rigged/our hand is weak/time destroys all we love/
we writhe in agony of the inescapable/all that is above/
will sink below/while we bellow/fume and foam/
ineluctable oblivion/back to dust and loam/
in the absence of god/we thought we were god/
we were nothing/savages dull and flawed/
high and noble/low and destructive/we wrought/
all for nought/we thought/all for nought/ all for nought/

∞

He who can command time commands the tides.
Earth's revolutions create a music to his ear as
The sphere
Careens through space and also through time.
He who can command space commands the sun
As we revolve through eons that feel infinite.
The seer
Knows that time and space are an illusion;
Dimensions are born every time we move,
But we believe only the three of space and
The one
of time, unquestioning, unknowing that space
Has seven and time has seven. We have forty-nine ways
To move but we sit in the dark and move to and fro—
To and fro—front and back, side to side. Ignoring
The ways
We must move through time like wrestlers,
Doubling it back, bending
Its sinuous fringes to our will, coiling its loops around
Our mind, through our mind, to see around the corner,
through the corner.

The trip we seem to always take is straight and narrow;
Timorous, pedestrian, uninspired.
Free our prosaic mind to see the options,
The odds,
Frightening as the profusion might seem.
Welcome the universe into your being.

First flood last flood
God no longer intercedes
The earth washes itself
Of dirty particles
Rinses scrubs and scours
Water sluicing down mountains
Down valleys down plains
Down to the coasts into the oceans
Who take the brunt of the sweep
Take the impure sludge down
To deposit in its depths of
Pressure and weight and endless time.

The cat who takes a bird
Never knows the cruelty of the
Forgotten nest
Where the fledglings wait
Under a useless sky
And wait
Hollow stomachs gaping beaks
Silent for fear of hawks
Unable to move frozen in time
Until flies find them through smell
And the rain washes out the
Loose feathers.

∞

Cruel Nature who sends the flood
Sweeps the animals down the mud
Down the valleys into the sea
Which can take quite a lot
Into its pressurized depths
Humans had a hand in it
But the innocent did not
Yet fur and feathers beaks claws
And camouflage mechanisms
All go down earth's maw
To the depths where none are saved.

Grow gills
        or die;
Remain unevolved
        then die.
The world is in constant flux,
Moving in tandem along fluctuant vectors;
        Life teems, swarms, seethes,
Constantly changing, maneuvering.
        It's the dance of life!
                But you sit this one out,
        And the next one and the next,
                Because you forgot how to move;
                        now you die

∞

∞

What will you do when the tidal hordes move in?
It won't be a monumental tsunami crashing on your head.
More like silent eddies of current coming in quickly to take over air.
Will you battle against the tide in a war you cannot win?
You'll tire and sink beneath the waves until struggle ceases.
Will you allow yourself to float out of your house?
The flow will take you far inland away from the coasts.
The water will take you far until all around you becomes a sea.
From one horizon to the next the sea spreads wide,
Until Sargasso meets Salish in one broad stroke of water.
You will float forever.

∞

La Ville Engloutie

Venice has known for centuries what man refused to believe
Ancient and beautiful palazzi whose flooded first floors
Made everybody move up to the second then the third
Fourth and fifth when they were there, rooftops when not

No more to be built on top when water laps at the antennas
TVs long engulfed and computers abandoned on desks
Beds made or unmade they'll stay wet for centuries
And all our plans and plots foiled by the simplest of elements
Water water water we should have known it would take over
Such an elemental substance that we need it to sustain life
Now it sustains and prolongs our submerged and hidden death

∞

∞

Le Pays Englouti

A vast inland sea
Reclaims its ancient bed,
From Appalachia to the Rockies,
The flyover country again drowned in flood and filth;
The nation divided once more,
This time east from west.
The heartland's under new occupation
By the newest ocean on earth.

The corn, the wheat, the soy, the cattle,
The Heartlanders, too, feed the creatures of the sea.
The slim coasts reconstructed as isthmuses from the north
Keep alive the Highlanders, but for a while,
Till they've consumed all their pets.

The rest of the world has nightmares, too.
No one comes to help the Heartland,
Its residents drove the world away eons ago.
For eons more, waves lap at oily, sooty shores.
No one remains to remember who lived there,
Or what it was to be the land of the free.

∞

Crustaceans in the liquor cabinet, sea anemones on bookshelves,
Fish inside cars protected from predators, expecting to be transported
But the motor's dead.
Barracuda charge down hallways, barnacles set up home on balconies,
Octopus lurk inside computers with broken screens, lobsters under beds
Dreaming they're asleep on pillows.
Sea urchins feast on our remains which underwater last but little
Shrimp take off with the rest but our hair remains,
Undulating in the new reefs.
Nobody wants our hair.

∞

The essence of water is to sweep clean
the muck of man
It can only be Earth's baptism, renewal, rebirth, man no longer
on its back
Man deserves his fate since his bibles, laws, and beliefs clearly
tell him convincingly
That he is the master of his planet, this orbiting orb that's never still
but which he clutches
To squeeze out her blood, rake up her dermis, penetrate her secrets
Till she's defiled
Stripped of her dignity, spoiled of her beauty, marred for her treasures,
But she reacts
Throws her usurper into the flowing waters of the baptismal font
After which at last
She reappears cleansed and pure, her seams closed, her quarries laved,
Her wells refilled
Her skin with new complexion glowing in the sun

∞

∞

I see things, disturbing things, when I look at you.

There's a cephalopod sitting on your head,
Inking your face, weaving its tentacles under your chin
Like a new Easter bonnet that pulses colors of neon;
Its molluscan foot anchors at the top of your skull
Where it drills to find soft tissue and feast on your brain.

You no longer remember your sin: you drilled through rock
Looking for fossil fuels that once were live tissue
And you took and you took till there was no more to take.
Then you found new violent ways to keep sucking like a leech;
You're so smart, now you wear the leech on your head.

It becomes you. It's you with electric hair. Its billowing tentacles
Search into your ears, slide up your nostrils, down your useless mouth.
There is food to be had in you. Up to the last second you denied
It was your fault; the torrents fell from above and seeped up drains,
Catapulted by rolling gushes across the sea to overtake the land.

"I am the victim here!" you howled, like the psychopath you are.
The water took you down. Lacking a conscience as you brought
Ruin to your home, losing memory of the crimes of your ancestors,
Faking blindness to ignore the wreckage of her whom you tore
To bits; her debris lying everywhere on land and sea accuses you, you,
you.

"I am the victim here!" you insisted, as the water took you down.
Don't you know, you're punished for the wreck you made of your home.
But as I see you now, you're the wreck: but hey you look swell
With that bonnet on your head. You tilt your head this way and that,
As if admiring yourself in front of a mirror that isn't there.

∞

∞

Water is a changeling: ice becomes water becomes vapor becomes liquid
becomes ice…

There are planets entire covered in water oceans
Whose waves lap at no shore and flow forever,
Their ripples circumnavigate the globes to eternity,
Prevailing winds the only force to move them.

Why the Earth should not join her sister planets
In becoming a liquid orb suspended between
One with burning gases, the other with deserts of rust,
Is a surprise to no one, save for the creature
Who thought the ground was made just for him,
Who believed that mountains and meadows were his alone,
Fertile valleys and even swamps were his to transform,
Change to his whim, drive the water away to some other place.

But water shifts, trickles, oozes, with a power he never understood.
When chased away from here, it reappears there,
Waiting for the moment to return with the full force of flood,
Or the treachery of a constant seep, a baby's whimper,
A drip-drip that falls or a silent current whose eddies
Barely move the objects they engulf.

Whole rooms are overtaken as their objects lie:
Keys on the counter, pans on the stove,
Books on the coffee table, birds in a cage,
A baby in its cradle, adults on their bed.

For centuries the tallest buildings dot the waterscape
Until only their antennas spear the surface,
Creating little circles of interference
As waves crest and trough around them.
Then, not even that.
The waves traverse the planet unimpeded and untroubled.

∞

∞

Our land was earned, chiseled out of rock, raised from muck,
By the healthy and the sick, to keep death at bay, grow babies strong
Who would pound and strike the ground at their own season.
Seasoned they came, fit, smart, alert, depending on themselves.

Where are they now, those smart-alecks who fashioned our nation?
There's none of them left to see and despair of what we have done,
How we misspent, mistreated, mishandled our bounteous inheritance,
Their legacy. Now that it's too late we've become dependent on others.

Others will act, others will try, others will swoop down to clean the air,
Bury the toxins or eject them out to space; some of us reject the obvious,
Deny what's wrong, refute the evidence, pretend our earth is eternal.
Yet we've sucked at her breast till her teat is dry, her chest caved in,
And still we dig our claws in and still we go down her arteries for blood.

Perforated, sullied, desecrated, our earth mother can take no more.
Without ire or blame, she will adapt to our ways,
Unleash the waters of renewal, clean herself from our filth and poisons,
Scrub herself of our cankerous cities, rub out our dependency on her.

∞

The say our earth is a living thing,
        her nucleus hot with seething fluids,
                her skies blue with generous gases.
Our earth is not dead like Mars or the moon,
        where sand, gray or red, decry a bereft sphere.
                The absent sky, or one that's withering away,
Serve a stern glare: our time might come when
        the green and the blue will bleed their hue
                to the gray of dust or the rust of rock.
Our last ones, the elders, will weep at our cruel governance
        that failed our earth, caused her colors to fade and bleach,
                one by one, turning life to gray, bleeding rich tints to burnt sienna.

∞

∞

When the earth groans, tremors seize her throats;
When the earth sighs, gales roar through her valleys;
When the earth shudders, continents move and split;
When the earth weeps, tsunamis collide and sweep all to sea;
When the earth moans, a soft breeze arrives to tell us she is dead;
When the earth gives her death rattle, a shroud of water covers her land.

∞

It wasn't enough to plunder your mother till she bled and trembled,
    You needed to murder your siblings for food and bloody sport;
Slash and burn her forests and jungles to cinder and ash.
    Dust and sand, wherever you go you leave just dust and sand.
Your lust for destruction makes your pulse hard and quick:
    You kill a sentient creature to make lucre of her tusks,
You domesticate and imprison whole species the better
    To devour them. Gristle and bone, that is all you leave.
Gristle and bone. Dust and sand. All you create is to take things apart,
    Dismantle, lay waste. What you discover as new and wondrous
Too soon loses luster and you cast it away, or abandon to die.
    You slaughter your own kind whether they are different to you
Or not. You betray others for no reason; you betray yourself as you
    Devastate your own earth, as if she wasn't worthy of you.
You do not possess the intelligence to feel your own shame,
    To weep for the blight, to regret your rapacity.
When the time comes that witnesses your own dying,
    With your last breath you might perhaps see that
It was all, all of it, due to your own greed, when you took
    And you took till there was nothing left to take.

∞

∞

Descartes snowbound had only his mind to entertain him:
    He wrote a book that many admired,
Look here, they said, in order to wrest nature's secrets away from her,
    In order to seize her and use her as our slave,
We must order our thoughts, create a body of science, be the master.
    Thank God the Bible taught us how to be overlord
Of all we see on earth: her body is ours to use and so are her other
tenants.
    She and they were created for us, only for us.
Science and religion combine to make us proud and overbearing.
    Our egoism knows no bounds. All is for us.
When we've used all we can use, when we've wrecked all there is to wreck,
    When we've taken and lost all there is to take and lose,
The earth will spring her last secret on us: she will terminate the virus
    That devours her and gives nothing back,
We are the virus who never learned the humility to be a fellow resident
    Of our earth, and she will shiver and send her seas on us,
To cover our shame and regret, to engulf our depravity and our
arrogance.

∞

∞

Go forth and multiply
So sings the word of god
in the book of books;
        don't question god:
sage, but rather odd,
keeper of wisdom, of sorts,
father eternal, if you like,
        whose paternal instinct is skewed.
Swarm and cover the earth
        he directed,
Until the earth can't recover:
lush turned to desert
bounty ravaged
magnificence undermined
your fellow creatures
        life's treasures
diseased, dying, dead.
This god—regal being—
is a wolf, overlord of nature,
whose might reaches horizons
like a blade, a scythe, a firestorm,
like you, in his image made,
whose destiny it is to cover the earth.
        You reach
the pinnacle and you stand
at the top of the heap as you look
over limitless horizons.
Sad that you crow your might
        and your everlasting right
On top of a dead
        and ruined
planet, maimed and killed
        by you
with the help of the mighty
        hand
of god.

∞

∞

Lepidopterist:
  You tried to pin her wings to a board of your making;
Taxidermist:
  Such an effort you made to stuff her and place her on your shelf;
Capitalist:
  With ease and for years you made profit selling her in pieces;
Geologist:
  You used your science to facilitate extraction of parts of her;
Creationist:
  With the lord behind you, the word was good to take possession of her;
Agronomist:
  You burned and slashed your way through her jungles and forests;
Chemist:
  With agrochemical biotechnology you poisoned her lands and rivers;
Sadist:
  You took pleasure in piercing her, in flaying her, in setting her on fire;
Scientist:
  You knew what was going on, yet you did nothing, or not enough;
Christ:
  Not a word, not a gesture, ever, in her defense, your silence proved
  murderous;

Mother suffered silently.
The patience of epochs is exhausted.
Still in silence and without blame, she will alter
Her aspect, change her demeanor, adjust her attitude.
She will send all these men to what is rightfully theirs,
The place they merit, for which they have worked for eons:
To oblivion.

∞

∞

Time and oblivion are the same: your artifacts will outlast you
    by mere centuries, a millennia or two.
After that, nothing. Your marvels removed by a renewal
    of the earth whose mantle never ceases to move;
Life will continue without you, even better without you,
    and the echoes of your lament will die in the wind.

∞

The history of your Mother is turmoil and upheaval.
    You chanced upon a moment of calm and stability
And called it permanent. You spread thickly over her skin.
    Foolish! Quakes and eruptions and tsunamis
Are Mother's tremors as her skin quivers during sleep;
    Her calm breathing brings snores and rattles.
Soon she will awake. Then you'll see your creations shift
    Into the sea and yourself out of kilter as her blood warms,
As she shakes her hair loose upon her shoulders.

∞

Consumers, consume your last before you yourselves are consumed.
As you devoured, you will be devoured;
As you fed, you will feed the sea creatures;
As you took without temperance, you will be taken down, away, apart,
Nothing was left after your voracity; of you, nothing will be left.

∞

∞

Fathoms and fathoms beneath the oil slick
Still stand, under great pressure,
Towns and depots,
Stations and Starbucks,
Factories boarded up and houses wide open,
Doors unlatched when frantic households
Ran for the streets, clutching deeds and photographs,
Insurance papers and beloved pets,
Only to be caught in the open
By vengeful currents that slammed
And threw their bodies
Under trucks and into trees
Where they hang like Christmas ornaments.
Their photos and important papers billow in the waves,
Flickering bits of light in the dark sea.

Only the tops of tall buildings dot the empty seascape,
Proof that entire cities lie beneath,
Like a shame to be covered or a blame
To be given: such was the fate,
Self-inflicted and self-generated,
By those who ignored all warnings,
Those who thought the planet was a
Christmas tree under which they could take
Its gifts and presents because they had the right.

The right is with them still, as bits of them
Hang and float away from cars stalled on highways,
From balconies and pharmacy drive-ins,
From factory windows and churches.
The vindictive waters swirl darkly around them,
Their grasping hands stilled and detached
From their overreaching arms.

∞

∞

Subterranean tunnels,
Boreholes. Drilling into her flesh,
Labyrinths beneath her skin like spider veins,
Open pits of festering wounds that ooze black blood,
Suppurating toxic gases into pipelines in swaths
A hundred feet wide, through forests that never knew
Such destruction.

Kindness absent, science disgraced,
Our Mother disfigured, her emerald mantle
Torn in tufts, her bedrock laid bare,
Her creatures banished, unable to survive
Our granite and shale nor able to drink
From muddied poisoned streams.

Drill and frack, spill and crack,
Kill, slice and gash: the parasite
Gives nothing in return, he only takes and takes
Till wells dry up and nothing's left to take.
Mar and destroy is all he knows, this thief
Who only steals his own future,
Knowing full well the things he steals
Will not last. Yet he can't stop
His clawing and mauling of the earth,
Going deeper and deeper with every technological leap,
Halting only when stone and dust are all that's left.

As Earth Mother lies with open veins and
Cratered pockmarks, ill with the disease of Man,
The parasite burns what he took from her,
Darkening her skies, belching forth poisons that rain on
Far-away forests and streams, increasing the kill.

Earth Mother bides her geological time.
When she gently shifts her mantle,
The parasite is wiped clear off her face.
In geological time she recovers, life returns,
Man does not.

∞

∞

frack-crack   wreck-rack
wreak-rock   work-torque
jerk-murk   stark-lurk
eke-ache   bleak-black
smoke-stack   stoke-stalk
stock-broke   coke-bake
break-risk   caulk-mark
dark-truck   tick-tock
sneak-fake   murk-track
trick-walk   trek-seek
balk-mock   muck-rake
weak-struck   freak-hack
chuck-crack   lurk-hawk
sick-berk   dork-folk
stink-wonk   dark-junk
crank-punk   reek-sunk
mock-mask   trick-sneak
slick-leak   stroke-choke
snuck-snake   sick frack
              wreck frack
              choke frack
              freak frack
              fuck frack

∞

∞

Measurement of Time

Science sees inside the second
With chrono meters and cameras
Set up to make time elapse in human scale:
A flower blooms, a drop drips, a nose sneezes,
In glorious color that's set to music.
Yet none has seen the electron move;
The photon's sashay remains in darkness;
Other queer particles move faster than a shutter's click.
They move, but they might as well stand still.

Strangler figs don't stand still: they send
Their spirals up towards the light, and down
Towards the depths, the darkest ones, where they
Seek to feed unseen in mulch or dirt. Humidity is
There for the taking. The human eye cannot see
The slowness of their reach. But if we leave,
Then return, with time and time, in the fullness
Of time, we perceive the growth, we notice the
Roots engorge, bifurcate, and flow like rivers of
Elephant trunks dripping down walls, engulfing
Turrets, settling on roofs that split with the weight.
Moss and ferns and epiphytes join the feast
Like vegetable guests on tile and quoins,
Greenery on stone, festooning man's works
With the entropy of nature, her indomitable weapon.

A tree, another tree, a copse, a forest grows
Where man had established his masterful dominion.
Who thought that temples reaching to the sky,
Settlements spreading to the horizon,
Roadways and waterways crisscrossing civil domains,
Would ever be dominated by leathery leaves,
Succulent tendrils, and sticky sap, thick and white,
Reclaiming with layered coats of resin the work of man,
Dominant once, but no match for the patience of time.

∞

∞

Time gives the illusion of life for breath follows breath,
　　Our heartbeat mapped out for us to see
As seconds tick by.
　　Sundials, clocks, watches, and chronometers
Help us keep the illusion alive
　　That logical life is chronological,
That we are alive because our timely dimension
　　Is as real as up, down, and across.
But time warps, speeds up, slows down,
　　Sometimes stops for a break,
Breaks our lives when it does,
　　Heartbeats stop, breaths become sighs,
Sight falters as light lingers while photons suspend their flight.
　　We see the flash, feel its heat on our flesh,
But the mind is mid-thought, cumbersome, half-asleep,
　　We see the image of the world
But we cannot know it comes before our birth
　　Or after our death,
Perhaps in-between at the moment we awake,
　　And we hear the comfort of the grandfather clock
Downstairs,
　　And we resume our life, slowly at first, with baby steps,
As we remember we're still alive, still breathing.

∞

What have we done with all that time?
We thought our moment in time was forever.
Turned out we were wrong.
Time moved and devoured us.
Our watches and clocks and chronographs
Were useless to stop us, the chronophagous hordes.
We and time were enemies, it turned out.
We couldn't see past it, and when the future came,
It surprised us, overtook us, made us decline.
Ebb and flow is the game of time, they say.
But no more. It is now we who ebb and flow.

Refraction is the bending of light through water
    Such a simple way to change what's there;
What does one call the bending of time through memory?
    Simple as well, but with great complexity
In its manifestations. We look through time
    As we see through water: we reach
For the image but nothing's there. We search
    Through time but it's all gone, our touch
Seizes nothing, our eyes ache for the past,
    We grow weary in our search for lost illusions.
We cry but underwater our tears are useless,
    The water engulfs our grief, our sobs soft and hushed.

Why do you insist on naming a savior,
son of god or god of the sun?
Does it matter who will not come
When time is done?
Who will not save man from his follies,
Too many to count, too many to pardon?
You won't be pardoned, either,
As you try to tend to the sheep.
The shepherd dies with his flock.

The time was when people noticed you,
Respected you, listened to you.
Nobody listens now, just as you don't listen
To the world relaying the information to you
That time is lost. Now death stares you in the face,
Yet you go on with your mundane concerns.

From gnomon to atomic clock,
Man has always craved the passage of time
And wished to become master of it.
Silly creature, thinking that by measuring it,
Dividing it into tinier and tinier increments,
He would get to possess it.

The way to become master of time is to let it go,
Forget it, ignore it, don't linger on it.
Move through the tenses of events as if they were one.
One only, the present. The past and the future move like a current,
But life in all its joy and grief is found only in the present.
Before and after, it's all out of reach.

Montaigne said it,
You of course don't know who he was,
        but he said it:
"Man cannot create a maggot, yet he creates gods by the dozens."
You who created your god in your own image,
        complete with penis,
Ask yourself: Why would god need this penis?
To create new gods?

∞

∞

Who is more powerful, god or time?
Is it god sublime and bounteous,
Who holds time in his hand,
Unspooling it at his whim
Or stopping it in its tracks?
    Sadly, no: it is time who directs god,
    Limits his actions, stunts his growth,
    Never lets him do what he wishes.
    Your efforts to keep him alive are in vain;
    Time will wither your will until it wastes away.
        It is time, don't you know, who lays down the law,
        Who leads everyone and everything
        To their natural end, their conclusion, their death.
        Including your important god: he will die when you do.

∞

Diluvium

Time is like a river, free-flowing, adaptable,
    open-ended, open to change, changeable,
    variable, fluctuating, ever-shifting,
    with the uncanny ability to find the least resistance,
    squeezing around obstructions with ease.
Time, the river, can flex and gather strength,
    to become a torrent, a flood, a deluge,
    a cascade, overwhelming the barriers
    and taking them down with it.
Time is now moving fast, too fast for some
    who don't see the gathering rivulet
    becoming a brook, a creek, a stream.
Time will not stand still for anyone,
    least those who beckon to the river of lies,
    the tides of misinformation,
    the tsunamis of fake news,
    all barriers that time will obliterate
    with its shattering momentum
    on its way to the sea.

∞

∞

No More Gods

Your time has also come to a sudden end.
No soliciting enemies to offend,
No driving back pagans, ejecting heathens,
You are out of time; there'll be no more seasons

For you to wander the wilderness, canvass
The neighborhood to thwart ungodly madness.
No Christ can help, no deus ex machina
In glorious descent like Zeus, Athena,

Or Thor, Buddha, Quetzalcoatl, even Ra:
They are mute, spent, impotent, and no more awe
Can ever rise from each degraded icon.

Kronos is the sole god left, the one who won:
The others kneel and bow, scrape and supplicate
For time to delay his sure and deadly rate.

∞

∞

Sunny bedroom
No way to block out the sun
Curtains are missing
Blinds were never there

One day the sun will be different
The bedroom will be lit darkly
Undulating light billowing light
Moving as waves across the floor

The thickness of water will serve as curtains
Only they'll move in sluggard fashion
Not with gusts of air but with currents
Swirling through the broken window

∞

Ode to Oil

Pipelines infrastructure revenue energy
Productivity oil assets growth logistics
Acquisitions returns crude margins statistics
Market share fossil fuels investors synergy

Development prospects strategy incentives
Networks human resource estimated profits
Operations earnings business guru prophets
Shipping trade investment power competitive

Forests trees meadows savannahs lakes
Swamps flowers butterflies bees snowflakes
Beauty color purity topsoil

Sunshine loam fauna coral reefs streams
Jungles beaches birdsong air. It seems
We lose so much for the sake of oil.

∞

∞

Fossil fuels
Are creatures that have been dead for eons.
There's not much of them left for us to use.
We will all sink to the bottom of the new sea
Along with our pets and gardens
And all together our bodies will provide the future fossil fuels.

∞

The ooze is a reddish brown, tinted gray at the edges
Where fish rot under the sun, jellyfish blue and pink
Caught in the sludge, their tentacles stilled, their bodies bloat
    and explode, adding their hot jelly stench to the
    complex of smells.

No nose can decipher that; nature didn't make the red tide.
It is all artificial: the nitrogen and potassium and sulphur
Released into the waterways, just so you can have your
    sugar in your coffee in the morning
    before work.

Fields of sugarcane wave in the breeze as if saying good-bye.
Green and healthy, but the run-off of chemicals that feed it
Flow down the river of grass, into lakes and streams
    find their way to the bay and make it
    toxic, toxic, toxic.

Ick tox, poisons and taints, turns the water red, turbid, fetid,
Kills the fish first, then it's the mammals' turn to die,
Manatees and dolphins, ulcerated hides, gray and dead
    float bloated on the high tides
    decaying fast under the sun.

∞

∞

Living within these walls
with the a/c on and the windows closed
I cannot hear the waves on the beach,
I cannot hear the birds hover over the waves,
I cannot hear the breeze rustle through fronds.
Only blaring car horns make it all the way up here
Where we're stifled like with cotton around our heads,
Processed dehumidified air blows across the room,
A far cry from the breath of the earth which from far away
Flows across distant lands and blows up and down
Through levels of sky, gaining degrees at the whim
Of the sun.

Long ago I saw the strata of sky, visible in colors,
As I descended into the airport at LA:
Blue at top, through orange, gray and pink, light rubbish red,
Then yellowish haze, greenish slate, and brown-flecked gray,
The color of nervous meat.
It was a marvel to behold, an awe that we could do that to our sky,
Make a layered birthday cake of it and hold it steady
So not even air can stir it.

We have cleared the smog, reduced emissions, banned hydrofluorocarbons!
But you neglect to see the harm that was done, the ruin of years,
The decay of centuries of burning carbon, peat, gas and oil in
Relentless and wanton burning, like fire on flame in combustive blaze
To destroy the fossils but create a new skewed realm of sky:
The very air we breathe transformed into tainted and foul winds
Able of holding color stacked from heavy to lighter bands.

∞

∞

Had we evolved quickly enough
    we should have had nostrils atop our head,
Sinuous bodies to move through water,
    flippers and fins and no hair,
Webbed fingers but no toes.
    Of what use are toes when deep in water;
Lungs, too, are a waste, for we should have grown
    gills.

∞

It's too late,
It's too late to do anything about the coming of the water.
Way too late to keep the oceans in check.
The time is up for our borrowed time
And now the earth wants its land back.
We consumed the natural, produced the artificial,
And now it's too late to collect it all back.
Too late to recall the soot that dirties the ice
And makes it melt all the faster.
Too late to save ourselves. But our plastic
            will last for eons and eons and eons.

∞

There never was much art in the artificial,
    just bad science.
Our artifacts multiplied by tonnage
    to drown the earth
    despoil its beauty
    maim and kill its creatures
    endanger human lives
    even killing us.
Materials that never were natural,
Plastics, styrofoam, polystyrene, gasoline,
    dioxin, DDT, solids, liquids and gases
To distribute to land, ocean and atmosphere
To make sure they followed us wherever we went
On earth, in the water and in the air.

I remember LA's air looking like a layer cake;
    now it's Beijing's turn.
Why so much poison?
    To make your grass green, make your car run,
Kill the ants in your pantry, make beverage cups,
    hasten the harvest, make garbage bags to hold
        all our garbage, our bountiful garbage.
We have so much we export it to China.

∞

∞

It doesn't take a naturalist
    to detect the changes in Nature,
no keen observer with high-caliber chrome tools.
    The naked eye is enough
to see changes from subtle to startling.
    Lend an ear to hear
reports from afar or from down the street.
    In your own back yard,
and into your home, creep in the clues
    that alert you to transformation
in the ambience, the atmosphere, the very ground
    on which you step, where you live,
where you nest, where you pursue your happiness
    and form irrational thoughts of permanence
and stability built on solid bedrock.

    But your bedrock is riddled with galleries,
empty shells of fragile calcium carbonate,
    an afterlife as transient as it is porous.
Solution holes of patient dissolution, sinkholes that
    swallow up your car and your house,
invading swamps crater after heavy rains,
    heavy rains, that linger long after their season.

The seasons extend, meld, interlace and fuse.
    There's no longer a time for dry or a time for wet.
Birds forget their travel, trees flower in error,
    millipedes invade your home, red algae blooms till it clogs,
corals die, streets flood, islands disappear, heat domes fester,
    hurricanes brood, ocean currents reverse,
salinity careens, humidity remains, clutching the heat close.
    We move through the air as we move through water,
heavy and slow. We will all have to learn to float.

∞

Herculaneum, Pompeii, Troy, Nineveh,
  Babylonia, Tikal, Atlantis:
Sentinels of witness to destruction
  and oblivion,
Time buried the rubble under
  mountains of ash
Or fathoms of sea, a dome of water
  to hide their shame from the ages,
Defeated, demolished, broken by temblors,
  incinerated by war or volcano
Drowned by rivers of time
  crisscrossing and double-backing
To make sure the remains remained
  hidden from view, lost to embarrassing looks,
Impervious to nostalgic glances and sighs of
  what might have been.
Dead and gone,
  dead and gone,
Dead and gone: your time went
  and is no more.
Shattered visage, collapsed atrium,
  razed palladia,
Swept beneath the rug of time,
  revealed in our time to gasps of horror
And spasms of recognition:
  They could have been us.
One day
  we will be them.

∞

The poems distributed at Flamingo Park.

∞

To a group of three men walking together by the basketball courts:

1A.
Two of you will live
But the third one won't,
Drowned like the rest.

Two of you love each other
The third one loves himself
But who of the three will be saved?

Two of you work hard to live
The third one never had to work
But will he be the one to go?

Two of you will leave
To go to separate places
The third will remain buried in sand.

The three of you are inseparable
Your destinies tightly entwined
Yet only one of you will stay and drown.

1B.
The three of you have known each other
since high school.
But two of you have been unfaithful to the third,
ousting him from your love affair.
He's on the sidelines now,
made into a third wheel.

But now one of you is in danger,
if not yourself, then the one you love,
or the one you don't.

Whom will you save when the time comes
and the danger is pressing on you all?
Will it be the one you love
or the one you don't?

If it be dark you'll not see
who is who in the maelstrom;
Beware the chaos for it might be you
slipping into the waves,
and one of the other two might be
the one who failed to save you.

1C.

The friendship you share
is troubling.
Your jealousy will be what threatens
the balm of bond and unity.

The three of you are linked by time
and familiarity, knowing well your strengths
As well as your faults.

The coming storm will bring you peace,
your resentful heart coming to rest;
Your spite and mistrust will cease,
but past your watery grave,
Your surviving pals will disunite
For shame and guilt will not let
their love survive.

∞

∞

To an individual lounging by the pool:

2A.
You will fly one day,
Up a whirlwind in a funnel
To the sky

Dark brooding clouds will crowd you,
But you'll see through the tunnel
A blinding light

Beseeching you to glide ever higher
And you pursue this flight from gravity
Unable to alter course,

The light air which you breathe fast
Will take you soaring,
Until it's hardly air you breathe last.

∞

To a couple walking hand in hand on 12th and Lenox:

3A.
Music is your soul:
    on the day of your death you will sing underwater.
French is your language:
    you will go out trilling your r's gutturally.
Your husband is your hero:
    he'll be swept out the back door while you're in the tub.

3B.

Your wife is your diva:
  on the day of your death she thinks you forsook her.
Your body is your strength:
  the water will eject you in seconds.
Love is your cause:
  the tides will take you inland, then out to sea.

To an individual getting out of a restaurant on Alton and 11th:

4A.

Outrun the coming waves
Outside your walls; this is my counsel.
Shouting won't stop them
Mouth open in wails to no avail

Flouting reason as you have all your life
Pout those silly lips to get your way
About face; you run up
Scouting old territory.

Doubt it will yield new directions
Out of danger as you flee mad and
Out of sorts; but up to you to
Outlast the floods

Outmaneuver the rising tides with
Outpouring of manic deprecations,
Outrage only you know so well,
Spouting epithets until the attic stops your

Outburst and the flood rises and you're
Outwitted.

∞

To a group of six men loitering in front of the Walgreen's on Alton and 10th: (There were five men initially, but one was still inside, and Iris knew it.)

5A.

You enjoy the view from the top: at 70 feet!
   The horizon extends to the ends of the earth.
Like a king, master of his domain,
      you smile at the miles of expanse,
the cardinal points exposed to your sight,
      The city basks under your delight.

5B.

How sad and ironic that at this locale
      you will meet your tragic end.
Fleeing the water you will halt at the top,
      but panic will be your guide.
You'll abandon your car
      to run the rest of the way.

5C.

Floods bar your way, you and your friends
      with a hundred others, strangers stuck, marooned
at the highest point of the bridge,
      the first day your hope is high,
with boats and ships frantic on the bay
      but no one stops; they search for others.

5D.

One of you dies fighting for water
    flung off the top where the view is magic:
cities to your left and to your right
    submerged to the second and third floors.
You see others congregate on isolated roofs.
    Are they dying, too?

5E.

One of you dies of depression,
    if such a thing is possible;
another one of you dies of heat stroke;
    still another of you dies when a boat
strikes the bridge and the piece that collapses
    takes you down with it.

5F.

The last two of you die of hunger and thirst,
    two of the last to hold on,
Watching a hundred others collapse.
    The dead litter the bridge from which
The view was breathtaking on a sunny day.
    Now all around is still, silent, and stark.

∞

∞

To a lady walking her dog on 9th and Lenox:

6A.

The dress you put on your dear Lizzy
clings to her fur and bogs her down
but your dead hand holds on to her leash

she drowns with you
     though you won't know her sacrifice

Let her go let her free no clothes or leash
she'll stay with you until that final day

you can't be saved but know that she can
if only you choose to let her go.

∞

To a man jogging on 9th and Jefferson:

7A.

You lean in and go the extra mile
Though you won't be able to outrun the waves
Your sight is keen your muscles strong
But you won't see nor very long outlast the waves
Your pulse is slow and your lungs in vigor
Yet against the waves your force will falter
Your well-shaped body entangled in kelp
In the dark recesses beneath the waves

∞

∞

To an elderly gay couple sitting on a bench on Meridian and 10th:
(A single poem for the two of them.)

8A.
You have been together so long
You move as one.
You anticipate each other,
You move in unison,
You cannot do otherwise.

You haven't said "I" in so long
You always say "we" and "us."
You will find succor when the end comes:
You will move together,
You will face the water in tandem,
You will be brave for each other.
You take courage from the other.
You two, you two, are inseparable.
You will fold your limbs together
You will hold each other tightly
You who only time can tear asunder.

∞

∞

To a man leaving his house on Euclid between 10th and 11th Streets:

9A.

Your house is your home
    into which you have poured your artistry,
    furnished lavishly,
    filled with objects of art,
    like a nest with which to catch a mate.

You've caught nothing so far
    but you aim high, seeking guests
    who share your esthetic tastes
    and who notice the Lalique
    when they sneak a peek.

But on that fateful day soon to be told
    your parquet floors will buckle
    when the water moves in, at first a trickle
    moving soon like a wave
    that catches the curtains and

Moves the furniture around the first floor.
    You climb to the second floor,
    but so close to the coast,
    You have no sanctuary.
    The waves follow up the stairs

Careen into the new areas with force
    chase you to the guest room
    where you will have no way out.
    There will be your sepulcher
    up at the corner of the ceiling,

As if you were one of your tchotchkes, bobbing up and down.

∞

∞

Loves Past Present and Future
The man you catch sight of today
    You saw in your dreams last week,
You just don't remember,

but the jolt of recognition is what catches your heart unawares
    as you make your way to see him, curiosity

Burns a hole in your imagination
    and crystallizes the intuition
that you'll befriend him. His voice is

familiar
as is his mien,
his way of looking over his eyeglasses,
his pupils dilating,
his nostrils flaring with every m, n, and ñ
which he pronounces in a gorgeous baritone,
nasal consonants that caress his lips, tongue and palate,
fricatives come to play, soft and resonating.

You want to lose yourself inside his pronunciation
Strain your muscles between teeth and uvula
Roll in the trill of his r's
        the thrill of his tongue peeking out with every
                voiced dental fricative: modo, usted, this, those,

Your heart beats faster, your blood gets thinner
The more he speaks, with a laugh thrown in to amuse,
        to bewitch, to dazzle with the vision of that smile,
                then you think that

all Argentines in the world are beautiful, attractive, sexy.
        You love Borges like you've never loved him before,
                Buenos Aires calls out to you as does Evita

from whose land he comes
and you want to feed him pastafrola and ñoquis and chocolates
    from Bariloche;
        you want to learn to dance the tango
free and
    passionate
and daring.

His lilt proves overwhelming and contagious,
    you speak with his intonation pattern.
You become his linguistic
twin,
imitating, wanting to be him,

or at least to kiss him: try
    to part his lips with your tongue,
explore the back of his upper teeth
    and taste the softness of his own tongue,
    feel the vibrations of his utterance

as he says, "I feel like I've known you
    for a long time."

∞

This Argentine, hairy and wiry as he is now,
    used to be French, very white, blonde, a woman.
Perhaps you remember her? She was your French teacher
    in Annecy, summer of '75.
She befriended you, interested in the Maya as she was
    and you from Quintana Roo,
        the land where ruins hide amidst the trees and
    ground cover, where the jaguar hunts and the
        quetzal flies its dazzling arcs against the canopy.

She died in Savoy, was reborn in Buenos Aires, this time a boy.
You met him for the first time, but he seemed familiar to you.
This is not the first time you've remet his soul.
Your avatars have been connecting for millennia,
    but this is the first time you've become this close,
        this intimate;
    the first time you've let your bodies unite.

That was new, exciting, a novel experience,
    one of mystery and exoticism. You trace his words
        like lines on paper: linear, sequential, logical,
    yet he has no idea of the tangential quality of souls, celebrating
        All Souls' Day with nostalgia and deference,
ignoring the fact that the souls are still all around him.

∞

∞

Love turns on a look,
on red freckles on a white back,
on a high noble forehead,
on eyes twinkling with intelligence.

Love comes from a carnal source.
Yet little do humans know,
    love is helped by the familiarity of the souls:
The longer they've known of each other,
    and the longer the contact,
The higher the propensity of love kindling,
    burning up a fever,
Heightening the ardor, ignited by a look, a smile,
    a sculpted philtrum.

∞

The pulse quickens,
-ing burn
    lust holds the body
-age host
Time is of no
-ence ess
    loses its
-ity qual
Eyes flare, pupils
-late di
Breath becomes
-low shal
Things lose their
-ing mean
Being in love means
    that blood is
-en molt

in veins that throb,
arteries that
-ten has
blood to brain,
-mage i
to mind and
passion to
-son rea

∞

Avatars cross paths
    with each other,
In time growing
    close,
Intimate as friends
    and lovers do.
In time they know each other well,
    they circle closer,
More intimate, perhaps
    members of the same family.
The time comes when they begin
    weaving in and out
In love and romance,
    passion and ardor,
Jealousy and devotion,
    oaths, duty and promise.
Yet, like all things confronting time,
    Their union might dissolve
And they go their own way.
    Avatars at times disunite.

∞

∞

You move too fast, too much, too soon.
You love too close, too long, too rash.
You wove your heart too strong, too near.
You dove too far, too deep, too brusque.
You clove too rapt, too strong, too much.

You scared him away,
You dared him to leave,
You snared him too close,
You spared no passion.

Spend your days now in solitude,
Wend your way all by yourself,
Fend off all companions,
End your days alone, utterly alone.

∞

The recognition of an avatar
        is not through the iris
                and onto the retina;
Image is of no consequence,
        appearance is deceiving,
                looks are of no use.
An avatar is recognized through
        that inner eye of the soul,
                that feels but does not see.
When your love from a previous life
        walks into the room, it causes
                your soul to bulge, to move,
To pull away and give you time
        to decide if you should move forward,
                since you've forgotten all the past.
Agitations that shook you to the core,

spill rancor and hostility for
love shared and lost,
For passions spent and hearts rent.
Perhaps your heart can take no more
from this particular passerby.
Yet, perhaps, your heart in valiant beating
quickens the pace in mad suspense,
"This might be the time,
This time will show us the way,
This way shall lead us to love,
Love that we sought, now seeks us."
Pull back, hide, flee; stand fast, observe, take the plunge.
Life is a mystery; the future, an enigma.

The death of a past lover leaves you cold;
Your blood freezes, not for the torment of the past,
Or the passion spent outside on hot, wet nights when
Jealousy made your limbs tremble as if they were cold.
Was the sand outside snow?
No, this present frost is for you and your curious detachment.
How could the passage of time weaken your fervor,
Staunch your fire, diminish your implacable sentiment?
Your fiber ebbs, your spirit wanes, your vigor weakens.
Years ago you would have died at the news;
Today you are dazed by your own indifference.

∞

Avatar Alphabetized
avanced in years and
   by experience forged, you
      consider with care the
         distance time allows to
            evolving kindred souls.

far you go into the past that
   guts all present moments,
      hollows out the future
         into empty probabilities and
            juxtaposes meaning with nonsense.

keen as you might be to
   love—love!—a false avatar,
      mistrust greatly your intuition:
         nothing is worse than loving some
            other who might not be the right

person, and worse, who holds up the
   queue and, woe, wastes your time,
      resulting in false starts, misdirection,
         squandered love, wasted efforts and
            troubled, deeply troubled, suspicions,

until the time comes to
   vanquish all pretenders and be
      with that one true love of the
         xeroxed, multiple avatar meant for
            you and only you through all your lives,

zigzagging and dovetailing with your grateful soul.

∞

∞

Pompeii

Even as Vesuvius shook the earth with its inexorable intentions,
Hissing forth fumaroles of sulfur and vapor,
Oozing necklaces of lava that writhed on burning grass,
Dropping pyroclastic rocks on streets,
People stayed.
The ground shuddered and the air caught fire,
The lagoon slopped about in its basin,
Thunder shook and darkness came,
People stayed.
The smoldering puffs, the wind-borne smells,
The first ashes drifting softly to cover the world in gray,
People stayed.
Sound muffled but the roar of earth's fissures strong,
Temblors excited the mind, flashes of light fired the nerves,
A few left, on boats, directly into the maw.

The explosion took everyone by surprise.
Too loud, too agitating, the earth caving,
Cracking, carving out tombs for the lucky.
The unlucky were there for the fire cloud
That swept them all to sea, while the
Flood swept them back inland.
Those that did not die by fire
Died by water;
Some died by burning air
Toxic that day.
The water, turbulent and black,
Swirled back out.
Ashes fell and buried the evidence hiding
The place of malevolence.

Today we survey the destruction,
The statues of people frozen in agony,
Mummies of ash and grit
Whose looks of fear endure
Under a blue sky spotted with flocks of white clouds.

∞

∞

Those who built houses in the west
    on the edge of the Everglades
knew the ground had been
    a swamp.
The tell-tale signs were still there:
    a land under the rule of water.
Those who outsmarted Nature
    built their houses on artificial
    berms ten feet high
far from a canal. False confidence!
    It is known how easily the water
    returns.
When the tides came their houses became
    perfect little islands,
Isolated as they were,
    no one came to their rescue.
The rescuers had their own problems;
    who could help?
    why would they come?
It was no man's land
    between the mire and the concrete,
first to be abandoned of all hope.
    The coasts had thousands of people;
The river of grass had very few.
    No one came.
    No one thought of coming.

Those who outsmarted Nature
    were terrorized in their isolation,
    waiting to live out their short lives,
    waiting to die
All alone.
    No one approached the horizon.

∞

Did no one see the signs?
Farmers knew their trees bloomed earlier,
    fruited earlier,
Deciduous trees changed their foliage earlier.

The turkey buzzards visited earlier, left earlier.
Painted buntings landed on bird feeders weeks in advance.
    The oleander caterpillar was at work a month before
it used to.
    Time seemed out of sync.
The weather brought forward
    the year advancing on its months.
The signs were everywhere
    for those who looked,
but no one looked,
    Save for a few
who gathered their surveys
    and wrung their hands.

∞

∞

The fable of the frog
    placed in a pot of boiling water:
        he'll jump right out with a seared behind,

But when bathed in tepid water
    that is but slowly turned up to a boil:
        he'll sit unconcerned until he is poached to stew.

This rather well describes man
    who sits apathetic in his tub,
        so unmoved and incurious,

Falling asleep, even, and dreaming
    that he is nature's child and reared in milk and
        honey and ambrosia and all the nectar in the world.

∞

Do nothing, say nothing, see nothing,
Observe nothing, research nothing, remember nothing.
Do not seek, do not know, do not notice.
The problem goes away, far away, into the night,
Into oblivion, into the world of the ignored.
Science will illuminate nothing here, in this darkness.
Yet the danger persists, threatening you more every day;
You decide to remain unaware, decidedly blissful, willfully oblivious,
Until she sweeps your world away and you along with it.

∞

∞

Selling the Future

Given to the CEO of a petroleum company whose oil tanker just collided
with another ship in the Gulf of Mexico:

You, who have been singing the praises
                              of the future
for so long;
You, who have hoarded divinely inspired
                              auguries
with rosy futures
     strong, marketable futures;
You, who have profited hand over fist,
                              fist over fist,
digging and scraping
     cracking and fracking,
          belching forth crude
and noxious fumes from which you make
          value
                              with dollar assignments
that translate to euros, yen and riyal
          better than the translation of words.
And when I put the conch to my ear
     I hear the sea
And when I cut up my credit card
     I smell the crude.
                    The plastic
Will last for centuries,
     accumulate in the ocean
          currents and eddies,
circling in huge swaths of debris:
                         a cesspool
     of foul and smelly trash.
It's what's left after the futures have been sold
          and cashed.

∞

∞

Eternity

Given to a clergyman leaving his church:

What you seek, what you long for,
    with every breath of prayer you make,
    is outside of time:
    you make time immaterial
When you say you want to spend eternity
    with God.
Who really knows about eternity,
    or even about God?
Where you live such statements abound:
    you bandy God and time about
    as if they were water and air.
    (Holy water and holy air.)
Why be so desperate to claim all of eternity
    for yourself and your flock?
Which other creature longs for extinction,
    believing that God and eternity
    are a duo to look forward to?
Religion may mute human curiosity in some,
    but the questions remain,
    unanswered,
    persistent in the dark
    and in the present,
    nowhere and nowhen,
    neither God nor eternity
    is explained.

∞

∞

Timely DNA

Given to a medical researcher in town for a convention on genetic disease:

Senescence,   they say
  is written in   the genes:
    that from the   moment you
      are born, the   stamp of time
        is printed on   spiraling strands,
        that from the   womb your doom
        is sealed, but   the place of your tomb
        is nowhere to   be known, is not encoded
        in DNA, in the   stars or in the sands.
        Ribonuncleic acid   etches on our souls
        parameters of growth   and decadence.
      In-between the inter-   stices is where
      we live our life,   scratching be-
      tween them to   catch a triumph,
    in a hurry to   express euphoria,
  beaten by the   game of slings and
arrows em-   bedded in the
  nucleotides   of fate. Serious,
    deadly game,   where the talents
    we receive in-   tertwine with afflic-
      tions as the   scroll unrolls its
        double helix.   We thunder and
      we despair,   struck and stranded
        by chemical   equations in a
        wizard's cauldron.   "Let me see!" we
          cry. "Let me under-   stand!" And "Let
        me see my master   who with a heavy
        hand wrests my des-   tiny from my well-
        intentioned plans!"   The chains coil
    around each other   to protect their
    secrets, while we   twist our back-
  bones in contor-   tions of fury and
pound on the   double helix in vain.

∞

∞

Inconstant Time

Given to a retired professor of physics, strolling in Flamingo Park,
enjoying the sunset:

Such confidence in your step!
Such competence in your eye!
Newton, Einstein, Fermi, Hawking
    prop you up and inflate you
So your skin is taut and shiny,
    your backbone ramrod straight,
        your head held high;
            you gaze to the horizon
              and beyond.

It's all a house of cards
    built on systems and funda-
    mental units and mathema-
    tical calcula-
    tions far from ac-
    curate.

Where you and your ancestors err,
    where the cracks appear,
    is in your apprehension of time.
Time is no constant
    and your attempts to measure it,
calibrate and tame it are in vain.
You keep adding seconds, ephemeris and
    Standard Internationale and leap seconds,
To make reality fit your scheme.
    But the earth oscillates, the
    moon wobbles, the sun staggers
    across space where everything

      pulls and pushes and strains
      against the laws of gravity,
fighting to escape and be free.
      But your earth is locked tight
      between a star,
      a gray rock,
      and an air planet,
just as we ourselves are locked into
        our fuzzy memory of the past,
        our tenuous grasp of the present,
        and our feeble expectations of the future.

∞

∞

Learning to Wage War

Given to a soccer fan, in town to celebrate his team's victory:

You sit you stand you sway you jump you wave
    you get so excited you want to jump the field
        to lend a hand

You shout you cry your rage you holler you whoop
    the adrenalin in your body
        makes your heart beat fast

This communion with your community
    is all that's left
A vestige of belligerence and warmongering
    of physical and psychological
Maneuvers around the tribal fire
    to increase zeal and vigor
To sharpen the hostility
    to stir up the martial passions
To determine the enemy
    and if there is no one
To invent one and accuse him
    of villainous crimes

Better your game than war
    even if you do want
        to kill your own goalie

∞

∞

Fausses Images

Given to a middle-aged gay couple from France:

Vous traversez l'océan
à la recherche d'une société
sincère et naturelle et pure
Vous vous êtes fait cette image
en lisant Rousseau—Jean-Jacques
et en regardant Rousseau—Henri, dit le Douanier

Les têtes pleines d'images du sage sauvage
habitant les vierges forêts
loin des boutiques et des cabarets

Mais vous êtes tombés la tête la première
dans une société où pullulent
les hypocrisies et les vaines fatuités
les vides patriotismes
et les orgueils creux

L'ignorance chez les Américains est comme un vaste continent
sans savoir d'où ils sont ou qui les a aidés
sans connaître le monde ou qui habite où
ils vivent sans conviction
quoique leurs croyances soient bibliques

Ils croient qu'ils sont les meilleurs du monde
ou peut-être même les seuls au monde

Le reste ils l'oublient ou l'ignorent ou le méconnaissent.

Alors pourquoi, semble-t-il, les admirez-vous?

∞

∞

Helios is No God

Given to a pale young man at the beach:

You've come from far away
from a tiny town near Toronto
where the war of seven years
    happened yesterday
No history happened
    when here
No one lived
    save for a few stragglers
    who left empty rings
    for us to observe

A place of no history is a place of no soul
    you think
So at night you're free to frolic
    not far-fetched at all
    to freelance your way
Inventing yourself anew
    with every person in your way
But by day you allow
    your life to be examined
by the sterilizing light of the Sun
    so bright that your
    deepest darkest corners
    are lit up
    lit clear
    lit immaculate

You think
the warmth of the Sun
    its brilliant heat
    its penetrating rays
replace prayer

You think
no sin is left hidden
    all is exposed
the light too bright
    you must close your eyes
    too dazzling to see
You expose too much
    like a bug in a lab

Helios shines like a god
You think
But Helios is no god

It's not light that
    shows your sins
It is time
    and only time
who allows us to see
    where and how
    and to whom
    we've transgressed.

∞

∞

What's Wrong with This Apocalypse?

Given to several severely religious people of different sects:

What's wrong with this Apocalypse?
What, no trumpet calls?
No parting of the heavens,
No descent of troops of angels,
No presence of a Supreme Deity?

The water will come in cold,
    and quiet, hardly a trickle,
    with miniature currents,
    little eddies around objects
    that float and bump against each other.

You wake up to strange flashes of light
    —it's the light of dawn
    reflected by the pool of water
    onto your ceiling.

You dash from the bed and step into
    the flood up to your knees.
    The cold takes your breath away.
    You stare at the water:
    it rises visibly.

You wake up the kids
    but then you wish you hadn't.
    They are not quite ready
    for the Apocalypse.
    They are not as ready as your are.
    But something feels off.
    Something feels weird.

There's no sound, save for
the whimpering and yelps of distress
from your children.

Where are the tolling bells?
Where is the trumpet blast?
Where is the symphonic music?
Where is the booming voice of punishment
and redemption?
Where are the wonders in the heavens
and in the earth,
the blood and fire and pillars of smoke?
Why is the sun dawning when it should be darkening?

Then you realize that you must die a horrible death.
The breath of life shall be denied you,
but the sting of death will not,
to you and your innocent children.
You call out the Supreme Deity's awful name
and you state that your repent,
but your brittle voice sounds hollow and muffled
as the waters reach your waist.

The time is nigh and the moment is here,
the moment you've been waiting for
rapturously.
Nigh is the time, but now you know,
you have to die
before you find out
if there is anything
—or anyone—
on the other side.

∞

∞

The underwater caves know
  how to be hollowed—it took eons—
  and then wait eons more
  for us to follow.
Emptied of ourselves we float like jetsam
  up the Gulfstream—we'll reach Iceland—
  in just a few months,
  like fish in a dream.
Our ribcage protects nothing
  our viscera unaccounted for—where's the pearl?—
  eaten by fish, probably,
  we are of no account.
We fall on the beach like bric-a-brac
  tibia interlaced with clavicles—my pelvis sank!—
  but vertebrae still strong, proud and interlocked
  like a bundle of fascicles
To be sent to a book museum.

∞

There is no one left. No one to take a last look,
cast a lasting glance, a wistful ogle, no lingering observation
to write down in a book of apocalyptic chronicles,
a narrative of the final moments of homo sapiens sapiens;
Sapiens? How sapiens was it that destroyed its own habitat?
Not wise enough, it seems, for wasn't the cataclysmic ending
foretold with plenty of time to avert? But no,
the species was as stupid as the dinosaurs who also
lacked plan b. No plan c, either. Although plan g worked
for the reptilian crowd: among them, one category survived,
and they took flight and conquered the air and the lands of all earth.
What will come of sapiens? Nothing it seems, because they
insisted on taking everybody with them.

∞

What kind of animal fouls its own nest?
A brute with no instinct of self-preservation,
Using, taking, using up, taking over,
Possessive, heedless, destructive, indifferent,
Sapiens as a name is irony and shame:
Where is the wisdom in what this species does?
No frontal-lobe planning,
No cerebral consideration,
No intuitive concerns over
The destruction of his mother
That leads to his own.

Now the earth moves on,
Her geologic time moves her spine
In a great frisson:
Mountains quake, seas move in,
Ocean currents stop, back up,
Invert their salinity equations as
Continents freeze, glaciers slide,
Deserts enlarge, encroach and hide
The sabotage of man,
Homo sapiens idioticus.

∞

∞

Roaches, rats and man
are Nature's errors: their sense of
limits is skewed, their sense deniable.
    They overrun their terrain and spill onto others',
        elbow and snout and antennae their way
            through and over and across and everywhere beyond.

They destroy as they go,
sweep and excavate,
tunnel into the earth,
    undermine the ground and poison it
        so nothing grows in it or on it or near it,
            and when it rains the poison spreads.

They plunder and they eat, always wanting always needing,
taking more than their share and spoiling the rest,
living beyond their means and bankrupting the earth
    till there's no more, till the spring runs dry,
        the oceans vomit up their dead residents
            and Mother is scratched raw and bleeding,

Wondering how she could have made such a mistake.

A creaking wakes you
The house under assault
An undercurrent of liquid
Moves like a creek
Illogic geologic chronology
You think as your mind is submerged
Quieted in its new oceanic milieu.

Your living room looks pretty
In this strange refracted light
Waves rippling shadows across the sofas
But the cushions are in such disarray
And the termites that you didn't have
Float over the coffee table and the Lladró
Picked off daintily by the new undulating residents.

∞

∞

Oolitic Limestone

Your historical home is solid—an original
    construction,
hewn from solid rock—coral rock—
    limestone.
But you ignore facts:
    oolitic sedimentary rock was layered down
by dying and dead things
off the coasts, an
organic muck
accumulated
through the
eons by drifts
of animal, algal and fecal
debris;
dead and
dying
things waft
down,
laying down
their tiny bodies
    to build
and build up
    masses of heaps, like garbage dumps,
fields of detritus that crush down
    the chaff of ages
becoming submarine hills
    of sediment death
using the dead to build up
tiers
and tiers
of lifting
mounds when
suddenly
they are
thrust up
in the air
as the waters

recede and
uncover the
work of
millennia.
    And land life treads upon it,
and man arrives and thinks
    —as always—
that the rock of dead things was made
    for him
and him alone.
    Man takes this rock
—as always—he takes and he takes,
    and hews it, chisels it
into blocks,
    and piles it into stacks
of wall that look solid.
    But the waters come anew,
this time hurried and propelled
    by man's meddling of earth, sky, and sea,
and the rock is home again,
    submerged
porous like cake dunked in milk
    and the water enters it
and bathes it,
    like old times,
ancient epochs,
    as the ages prepare
once again
    like innumerable
times before
    for their infinite
and patient
accretion
of new
sediments
of higher
life forms
of dead
and dying
things.

∞

∞

Housekeeping

Nature has a cataclysmic way
    of keeping house
    of sweeping things under the rug
Cyclonic winds and seismic waves
    pelt the creature's habitat
    crack it up
    wipe it all away
    to her satisfaction
The coasts are clear
    as well as the new inland sea
    which swept the plains clean
Now for the mountains
    to the east and to the west
She hunkers down and shudders
    unleashing temblors and fire
    that exceed the floods in power and awe
Until all evidence is bulldozed
    and cleared away.
No parasite ever lived here

∞

Industrial explosions, accidental fires,
chemical spills, accidents on railroads and highways,
toxic gas releases in ribbons and plumes,
hazardous waste seepage into ground water,
they all happen
by accident, negligence, incompetence or indifference,
they happen.
Disasters are inevitable
where man is involved.
He produces poisons, stores them,
transports them, unleashes them.

No danger is too risky
so long as it makes money.
Lucre is more important than life,
than health, than well-being,
than peace of mind.

The vast horizon, were you to see it,
is of turbid green water
with splashes here and there
of red algae blooms.
Breaking the surface of the water
like uneven candles on a
lopsided birthday cake
are the taller buildings,
a funereal procession of
tony addresses marching
into the distance.
But you won't get to see it.

 Gaia

Gaia, my love,
Trembling planet in the cold of space,
You travel in ellipses, spirals and vectors,
Wobbling in circles around yourself, hurling
Around the Sun, gyring on an arm of the Galaxy.

Yet you had time for us,
Terra genetrix,
The magic of life sprouted
And out came us,
Your most dangerous organism,
Because we kill the others.

∞

You will die electrocuted in your flooded apartment.
The machine you wear at night to help you breathe
Will take your breath away.
It makes so much noise
That you hear nothing as the waters
        rise
Toppling chairs downstairs, breaking
Windows, creeping up the stairs.
When the power cord gets wet
At the outlet
With the water
        rising
It sends electrons up the cord
Down your trachea
Your torso will
        rise
In a final cramp of pain.
You will never feel the cold water
        Rising
To cover your body.

∞

The youngest one of you,
A daughter,
Will survive because she is off at a slumber party.
The remaining ones will go together,
As if you were in a pool,
But in your family room.
You will go together yet apart,
Because at the end
You all separate desperate for a way out,
Clawing to find a pocket of air,
Perhaps up at the ceiling.

But all you find is unforgiving plaster
Which you manage to scratch off,
But just a little.

You have recently moved in.
A house built to your specifications,
Beautiful, spacious, expensive.

Still not a tree in the garden,

But you have plans,
Lots of plans.

You should have filled up the fridge,
had you known.

With nothing in it
It will begin to float
With the coming of the water

When it floats it overturns,
Pinning you to the wall

You cannot move, save for one outstretched arm and its grasping hand
But it grabs nothing.
It cannot stop the water.
The hand moves in frantic circles
As the water moves up and up.

∞

Asleep in bed
It surprises you when the water comes
Lapping at your duvet
The cold wakes you
Awake wide awake
Adrenalin flowing inside like waves
Of panic lapping at your lungs
Alert but not smart
You open your back door
Letting the rest of the water in.

It sweeps you back into the living room
Where you cannot fathom what is happening.
You drown wondering what it was
that killed you.

∞

The walls of your house will collapse
and the roof will fall in
Consider it a blessing
your death will be faster
            than drowning
much easier since you won't have the time
            to think of the children
in the room next door
They'll go from sleep to nothingness
Like they go from a lullaby to sleep
Lulled to sleep
Lulled to death

∞

∞

Your penthouse on the thirty-sixth floor
will buy you time.
You will see the rushing water encroach from the beach
overtake the pool, the patio, topple palms,
float the cars away from the parking lot.
They bob up and down like colorful rubber ducks in a tub.

You will have the time
to observe all that happens
in your domain.

The sun will rise and set many times
on the flooded plain,
no way to tell ocean from land.

You go down to check your boat
in the marina.
It is nowhere to be seen.
The view from down here is heart-wrenching
and the stench of death overwhelms you.

It takes an hour to get back upstairs.
You never again will go back down.
You debate if a bullet to your head
is better than waiting until the food is gone,
the booze will last longer, but that's no sustenance.
And just how will you boil the water?

In the end, the water will call to you,
Lovely sirens hidden in the waves,
to lure you, beguile,
and you, smitten, will jump from your balcony
in order to meet them, to be with them,
swim with them and have them caress you.

∞

You will have heeded the signs
    but not soon enough
The water will catch you on the expressway
    where the tide moves faster than the lines of cars
Many abandon their cars driven now by the tides
    but you'll stay in yours because
You never learned how to swim
    surrounded by water you feel the pressure
You remember hating the pool or beach
    and picnics for that matter
Too much sun and too much heat,
    the salt in the sand stings
Now you wait for the water to lap up
    past the windows
The car floats and then you're a child again
    at the carnival playing Bumper Cars
As all the cars go careening
    off the expressway and on
And on.

∞

You're a night owl
Cannot sleep
Stay up all night
Hardly sleep

On a night of a full moon
Swirling reflections on the street
Call you to a window
The ground is moving

Your eyes cannot believe
That it is water advancing
On the neighborhood
You think of California mudflows

Hawaiian lava flows
Javanese lahar flows
Until your mind finally clicks
Onto the right cataclysm

Japanese tsunami
At your back door
Up and over the patio
Into your windows

Down the wall
Across the floor
Around your ankles
Up your legs

The cold wakes you
From your paralysis
You start to run
But with water to your knees

It's hard
Still you go out the window
Thinking it's safer out there
But when your feet

Hit the ground
The current sweeps you
Off them and
Carries you away

Into the street
To join the mass of
Flotsam streaming along
Bobbing and wobbling

In colorful disarray
And all you see is
Seething and churning
Around your human head

Unprotected
The cranium bones
No match for the rage
Of the tumbling waves

∞

∞

The Bad Neighbour

Karma is a close cousin
        of Kronos:
You of all people
        who never once
        cared
about cultivating friendships
        or sowing good will,
        should know.
You'll reap a solitary death
        shunned in your
        hour of
        need.
Your McMansion strong
        as a fort
        will crumble in the
        waves
Falling walls follow you
        down the
        stairs
and out the front door.
        You thought your house
        indestructible,
        you thought your house
        firm solid tough
but it all sweeps away
        while you watch
        from the top of your car.
It is huge and gas-hungry
        and it floats away
        in the swirling water.
Your neighbors watch
        your car bobbing in the

current
as you struggle to stay
on top.
No one comes out
with a look of
concern.
No offers of a helping
hand
and when you tire and slide off,
your neighbors sigh at
what it took
to finally get rid of you.

∞

A Tourist's Last Day

While on holiday,
a respite from the cold,
days at the beach, nights at the club,
on such a solid day
as your last, you are overfed
and overly drunk.
No thoughts on the end of days
even when the hotel trembles
from the onslaught of wave after wave
that take the lobby out the back doors
and into the pool.
High up you hear not a thing
of the clatter and thundering sweeping
as the tides overtake the ground floor
then the second where the first residents
start to drown high up near the ceiling.
You keep sleeping as if on a cloud
Until screams in the hallway wrench you awake.
Was it a dream? No, the hubbub passes your door
and you spring up, remember to step into your slippers,
wrap your robe around your nakedness
and stealthily open your door. No more noise.
What was all that about?
You close the door, go back inside.
Curiosity makes you go to the floor-to-ceiling window.
Twenty floors below you the world is careening and
sliding off-kilter, and you smile: the window is a computer screen
there to entertain in the middle of the night.
Your mind does not comprehend what is real.
Your heart remains calm,
but when the room creaks into a new angle
and the bed careens towards you and presses you to the window,
then it begins to seep into your mind.
You have the best view in the house
As the building topples onto the maelstrom below.

∞

∞

Predator

You don't recognize yourself as a
   predator;
Others do the job for you
   —The pay
is handsome—
   you give every day.
For convenience,
   your meat
encased in plastic
   has no gristle, nerve or bone,
ready for the fire
   to be cooked.
To be consumed.
   To be devoured.
You never thought of yourself as prey
   but the coming of the
Water places you at eye-level,
   cruising in graceful indolence
while you splash and spray
   calling for attention
—as you always do—
   and the unblinking eyes
just above the surface,
   followed by rows of tough-hide
ridges that end in a
   tail of sinuous swish,
accommodate your bleating,
   your splashing.
Might as well ring the dinner bell
   to announce that
dinner is served:
   crudités au jus.
Not very refined,
   not served on bone china,
but served with gristle,
   nerve and bone,
and quite a bit of hair still on
   the better cuts.

∞

The birds are all gone
Replaced in the trees by cats and dogs,
No one to rescue them.
Even humans wonder
Why no one comes.
They can't see how far the floods go,
    from horizon to horizon,
The water stretches farther than the eye can see.
A few who hope and have a boat
    brave the stretch of bay
Where leisurely they once floated.
Now they bounce on debris
    amidst rafts of floating dead,
No safe harbor now,
    no place to go,
    cannot go forward,
    cannot go back,
A new river Styx
    that even Charon cannot cross.

∞

∞

The Weight of Water

Neptune's child is not the Kraken
for it is rather a local monster.
No, the monster who sleeps
Awakens drop by drop, each a tentacle
reaching towards the sea to add
    its weight in flows and currents.
It is the ice, frozen in place for eons,
    which stirs, in rivulets and eddies,
Adding drop by drop, drip by drip,
    to the volume of the sea.
The Whiteness is gone, which reflected to space
    the sun's rays that now penetrate deep
into the soil and the warmth seeps down,
    the tundra is unlocked
and releases the water down
    the land and into the sea
      the swollen   sea
the rising   sea, heavy   with
    movement   liquid gravity
dancing   with winds   bracing
    with breezes   ocean cliffs
    flowing down
southern   latitudes and
    throwing their weight   onto   the coasts
      tentacles moving   in wild
directions   covering   covering
    a liquid   lid, heavy   and thick.
The Kraken   has been   released
    everywhere   at once.

∞

CPSIA information can be obtained
at www.ICGtesting.com
Printed in the USA
LVHW092011300919
632708LV00007B/175/P